Resurrection
Shifter Chronicles
Book 2

ANITA COX

DEDICATION

To my awesome fans, who have stuck it out with me,
waited for new projects, and keep me laughing daily.

I thank my wonderful family who live with me staying up
late into the morning, ignoring your needs so I can write,
and for proudly announcing that I write smut. I love you
with every molecule of my heart.

And always, to my friend, Houston Havens. It is such a
beautiful thing to have such a wonderful friendship with
someone who understands this life. I enjoy our
conversations about everything from aliens to herbal
remedies. I love you and Mr. Havens to pieces.

ONE

Wendy, sister to the retired Alpha of the Belfast pack, Colin Baker, sat in the conference room where she waited for her new Alpha, the first female to rule in centuries. In silence, she nervously eyed Roman and Grace LaRossa, King and Queen of the Lycans, sitting across from her. Smoothing the sweat from her hands along her pants, she reached up and tucked a loose tendril behind her ear. Swallowing hard she found her courage and boldly focused her stare on Grace, who she knew would be more apt to explain. "Do you know why I was summoned here?"

"You're not in any trouble, Wendy, but Nala asked to be here for the conversation. Take a deep breath." Grace's sympathetic smile spread across her angelic face.

In an effort not to fidget, Wendy folded her hands and put them in her lap. She'd always gone above and beyond to serve her pack and couldn't imagine she'd done anything to be summoned by the Alpha. Nonetheless, here she was, heart pounding in her chest, shirt damp with sweat as she waited.

The conference room door opened, Wendy shot out of

her chair. Her brother Colin walked through first and held the door for his wife, the Alpha. Nala was a stunning exotic beauty; about six foot two with mocha skin, dark brown silky hair and chocolate eyes. If the fact that she was an Alpha didn't intimidate, her appearance certainly did.

"Wendy," Nala said with a smile, "please sit."

She reclaimed her seat. "Can we get to why I'm here please? My stomach is in knots."

Colin shot her a look that said to be patient. She glared back at him, grinding her jaw.

"You know, the school is nearing completion?" Grace began, breaking the ice.

Wendy nodded and twisted her fingers. *What does that have to do with me?*

Nala grabbed Colin's hand. Wendy felt as if her eyes would fall out of her sockets. It was an arranged marriage and the two had been cordial at best, at least to her knowledge. Clearly things were changing.

"Why don't you tell your sister?" Nala patted Colin's hand encouraging him to continue.

He leaned back in his chair and looked at Wendy. "You know, you said something to me once about finding your mate."

"Holy hell! Are you marrying me off?" Her mouth fell slack as her heart raced. She'd always hoped to find love and a bond she had coveted for so many years. *How could he do this to me?*

"Jesus, Wendy. No!" He shook his head and squeezed his eyes shut for a brief second. "You have been such an asset around here for so many years. You're very organized. It's natural for you to care for others. You look out for all of the younger Lycans. You have counseled me so many times. You're stronger and smarter than you realize. Perhaps, we are holding you back."

Grace slapped Colin in the arm. "Quit torturing her." She turned to Wendy. "Hon, would you like to be

Headmistress at the new school? We think you could serve the students well. Plus, with other Lycan professors…you never know if you're gonna find a hot Lycan to sweep you off your feet."

Wendy's face burned hot with embarrassment. "So this isn't about my abilities as much as it is about my love life? I'm seventy-five, not really the age for new beginnings." Her heart was in her throat. What were they playing at? Seventy-five was young for a Lycan, but still…she wasn't exactly a pup.

"No, Wendy. It's just that…we think you might enjoy expanding a bit. Get out there, meet others." Nala cleared her throat. "You are always welcome to stay here and continue what you're doing. But I see strength in you—a rare kind of strength and wisdom. I think the young adults at the university would benefit wisely from your presence." She scooted her chair back, the legs scraping against the floor piercing the air like the cry of a hyena before she stood. "I have the utmost respect for you, Wendy. This is your choice. Not an order. Take some time to consider it."

Nala's exit from the room was swift, leaving Wendy staring at the vacant door before looking back at her brother.

Colin frowned at her and shook his head. "Don't be difficult."

"Bite me," Wendy said with a huff as he tucked his hands in his pockets and strolled out of the room. He may be the Alpha's mate but he was still her little brother.

Roman, who hadn't said a word, reached across the table and grabbed her hand. "You've always been there, been *here*, for me. Grace and I would be delighted if you'd move to the school with us. But I know, first hand, the devastation that comes with even thinking about leaving your pack. Whatever you need, Wendy, know that Grace and I are here for you." He gave her hand a gentle squeeze before releasing it.

"Yes we are," Grace chimed in.

"Thank you." Bewildered and confused by the mere idea that they'd dare to ask or even wanted her to leave, Wendy shot out of her seat so fast, the top heavy chair crashed to the floor. "Excuse me, please!" In a hurry to flee the situation she didn't even attempt to right the chair before she bolted from the room.

As fast as she could manage without making another scene, she swiftly made her way out of the house and to the woods. The air around her shimmered; like water in the sunlight, as she shifted to her wolf form. Stretching her front haunches, then her back, she set off at a trot. How could they ask her to leave? This was her home; her family…a musky scent wafting past her nose on a zephyr breeze making her stop at a log and sniff at the muskrat hiding inside the hollowed old tree. She decided to leave him be and continued down the trail to the lake. The early morning light pierced through the pines, casting a bluish glow in the forest that spilled out onto the water reflecting a silvery shimmer. Plopping on her hindquarters at the water's edge, she hung her head with mixed emotions. After seventy-five years, the view was still breathtaking. Did she really want to leave this all behind?

This was her home. She'd never left their territory and the thought of doing it now terrified her. Having her brother remind her how lonely she was, did more harm than good. What if she made the move and still felt lonely—worse yet, that the loneliness would be amplified by foreign surroundings and lack of a pack for support?

At her age, she was starting to show signs of aging, which shouldn't happen for another hundred years. It had puzzled her immensely but also troubled her. Who is going to want an ancient looking Lycan for a mate? Nature could be a cruel bitch.

"Mind if I join you?" A deep male voice had shaken her from her thoughts.

Spinning on her paws she released a growl until she saw Zoltar, the Centaur King standing on his hooves. He quickly shifted to human form. "Whoa girl, I didn't mean to startle you." He held his hands up, in mock surrender. He was a visiting dignitary, frequenting their pack's land during the construction of the new university.

She quickly shifted, joining him in human form. "I'm sorry, Mr., uh, Mr. Zoltar. I, uh—" Why was she stammering? She looked up at his bronzed skin shining beneath his golden curls that spilled over his face in such an enticing way every single cell in her had ignited with lust. *Damned Centaurs always send our hormones on fire!*

Giving a seductive shake of his wheat-colored locks, he gracefully reached out his massive hand. Feeling nothing but a strong draw to him, she stretched out her arm in offer of a friendly shake, but he incased her fingers into the warmth of his palm and drew her hand up toward his sculpted lips. Her heart fluttered with excitement as he lowered his head pressing his soft mouth against the flesh of her knuckles while keeping direct eye contact with her. His voice wrapped around her like chocolate embracing a cherry. "My sincerest apologies for startling you."

Her nervous belly flopped inside as she tried to fight off whatever spell she was under. Her knees felt wobbly and heat began to radiate up her neck to her face, which she was certain burned red.

"Please, just call me Zoltar." He smiled down at her, his fair-hair glowing in the light of the sunbeams peeking through the trees. "Mind if I join you?"

With heat still stinging her face, she walked past him. "Certainly." Reaching a large stone, she sat. Though she heard him following, it was his distinct aroma with hints of cinnamon and vanilla that tickled her nose, telling her he was very close, maybe a little too close behind her. She could feel the heat radiating off of his skin as he sat next to her. Not knowing what to say, she resumed gazing at the water.

"I discovered this place the first day we arrived. Once I saw the beauty of the morning light, I've longed to revisit."

He leaned back, placing his palms on the stone. He closed his eyes and took a deep breath through his nose. "The smell of the morning dew is like heaven."

While his eyes were closed, she took the opportunity to look him over. She traced her gaze over his lean arms and muscled chest—his T-shirt hugging every ripple. Averting her eyes before he caught her, she straightened her head glancing back toward the water.

"I couldn't agree more," she choked out, gaining control of her wayward thoughts. "I love the smell of the forest waking for the day—that earthy, sweet aroma. It calms me almost as much as the sight of our beautiful lake."

Leaning forward, he plucked a lily and held it toward her. Once she looked at him, he flashed his brilliant white teeth. "It's not the only beautiful sight this morning."

Her heart skipped a beat. The first time she'd seen him at the meeting with the other clan royalty, she'd frozen in her tracks—awestruck by his unique looks. His face was breathtaking. And he'd noticed her staring at him, though he'd not said a word since.

Just like now. She couldn't utter a word, but only stare in disbelief of the words she knew she could not have heard right. She forced herself to look away. Centaurs had a draw on other species. No one knew why, exactly, but their mere presence set the females to acting like they were in heat. A fling was the furthest thing from what she wanted or needed. What she desired more than anything was her own mate. An older Lycan woman with a Centaur was almost a guarantee of never bonding or procreating, unless, of course, you were looking to incubate a Centaur baby.

The thought brought about a dark shadow of sadness. Wendy wanted a family. She loved children and had the natural desire to nurture. It was fate's cruel joke refusing her a mate and preventing her from loving and having children of her own by now.

"I can't help but notice you look lost in thought. Is everything okay?"

Wendy turned to him again. "I've been invited to be headmistress at the new university."

His laugh was smooth. It flowed like melted chocolate, stirring her longing further than it should have.

"It means leaving my pack, Zoltar. That's very difficult for a Lycan to do—especially one my age." She looked down at her feet. "An old handmaid sure, but I'm very attached to this place...to my pack."

Standing from the rock, he extended his muscular arm toward her, his fingers relaxed and open. "Walk with me."

After considering him for a split second, she complied, though she wasn't entirely sure why. She wanted to sit and ponder her future, not wander around with a Centaur who would surely try to seduce her. Still, she followed him down the path around the lake, hoping no one would see them together and start gossiping about her desperateness for a mate. The Lycan men were on edge when the Centaurs arrived and the Centaurs had sworn an oath to keep their hands to themselves.

Wandering around alone with a single Lycan female wasn't exactly part of that oath. Wendy's hopes of finding a mate could be completely devastated if the men thought she was sneaking off in the woods with a horny Centaur male...King or not.

"How much do you now about my race?" He looked at his feet as he walked, his brows pulled together.

Shrugging she turned her attention to the path ahead of them, not daring to gaze at his handsomeness—a potential distraction. "Same as everyone, I guess. You have the ability to seduce females of other species so you can produce more Centaurs...being that Centaurs are only male. You are powerful warriors, fierce in battle."

He strolled in silence for a moment, nodding as she spoke. "You know, there is far more to us than that."

"I'm sure there is, Sir." It was a fine line to walk,

keeping a Centaur in check while managing not to be offensive at the same time. Anxiety teetered at the pile of emotions overwhelming her.

"Zoltar, please," he corrected tilting his head. "Or you can call me 'Z' as my friends do."

"Z?" She giggled. "How new age."

He smiled then looped his arm in hers as if they'd been friends for ages.

The warmth from his arm permeated through her, giving her an odd sense of elation. She swore she'd have to remind herself to breathe.

"We are the sons of Apollo."

His words caused an unexpected chuckle to escape her lips once again. "It explains the good looks." Silently, she chastised herself for that statement. How dare she flirt with him?

"I find it very pleasing you think so," he said with a wink. "It is true, we are fierce warriors. Fierce, but not invincible. The last female Centaur was killed in the battle with the Lapiths. There has yet to be a female born to our kind. It was our ancestors' pleas to Apollo allowing us the ability to breed with other species so we would not go extinct. *However*," he cleared his throat, "our offspring are not a hundred percent Centaur. They can shift into the form of their mother as well."

"What? You're telling me a child could shift to Lycan *and* to Centaur?" She stopped in her tracks. "How is this possible?"

Releasing her arm he turned to face her. The air around him shimmered and he shifted into a golden wolf briefly before shifting back into his human form. "Yes, it is true."

She gulped. "Well, Z, if I needed a distraction, you certainly came through for me."

He bowed. "Now," he looped his arm in hers once again, "we are also very good at Astrology. We all have individual strengths, as I'm sure Lycans do. I, for one, have a touch of precognition. I'm also a bit of a healer."

Shifting his eyes, he glanced at her while keeping his head forward. "Care to know why a Lycan of your age looks quite a bit older?"

She could not hide her embarrassment. The desire to jerk her arm loose and run far from him was overwhelming—or perhaps she could crawl under a rock. "Nothing I can change, so why bother?"

"And if one simple kiss from me would turn the clock back for you, would you grace my lips with yours?" He didn't slow his pace as he waited for her to reply. When she tried to jerk her arm free, he held on a bit tighter.

"What? No." She wanted to go back to the house, away from Z. She wanted some space so she could focus on the problem at hand...the university, her brother trying to get rid of her, being hopelessly single and aging.

"Your beautiful hair, restored to its former glory, the worry lines erased...the only cost being one simple kiss?" He laughed. "Does the thought of kissing me repulse you *that* much?"

"No." She finally pulled her arm free. "I'm not some young pup you can trick into your bed." She turned her back to him and started off toward the main house. His long legs prevented her stomping pace from putting any distance between them.

He latched onto her hand. "Please. I did *not* mean to offend you."

She stopped, causing him to bump into her. The heat from his body sent her senses on fire. She could smell his arousal, meaning he could smell hers. She silently groaned. "Look, I don't know what you're playing at." He was so sexy, standing there in a pair of jeans, hanging low on his hip. His blonde curls bounced when he moved.

"Fuck it." She meant to give him a quick peck to shut him up, but something else happened. When she stood on her toes, large warm hands cupped her face. His searing lips brushed up against hers, making her limbs feel like putty. Her ears started to ring.

The kiss was slow and tender, but quite respectful. He didn't shove his tongue in her mouth. He didn't crush her mouth with his. This…was a first kiss, a tender moment and it melted her.

When he released her, she felt heaviness in her lids.

"That wasn't too repulsive, I hope."

Staring at him, she was at a loss for words, or a singular thought.

"I see," he said with a smile, the thought of rendering her speechless apparently entertaining. "Race you back to the house." Shifting into his wolf form, he tore off, leaving her behind. Wendy shook her head to clear her mind before shifting and taking off after him. His wolf was large, nearly as large as Grace's. Wendy figured it had something to do with the royal blood. However, he didn't spend much time in his wolf form and it was obvious as he was rather slow.

Wendy pushed hard to get next to him. He looked over at her and made a leap to get ahead of her. She dove under him, digging in her hind quarters then sprinted toward the yard, which was only a few feet ahead. When she finally skidded to a stop, the large Centaur-Wolf was skidding up behind her. The both shifted in unison.

"You're a vivacious runner, Wendy." He nodded. "Very impressive."

"Wendy!" Colin stood glaring at Zoltar. She'd just been caught cavorting with a Centaur…by her brother.

.

TWO

Nala had insisted Wendy join the table and let some of the other pack mates serve for a change. Wendy was certain it was supposed to be a kind gesture, but it made her feel so much more out of place. She had to sit and stew that Colin would make a federal case out of her run with the Centaur King.

"Wendy?" Grace called to her from across the table. "We are going up to take a look at the progress on the school's dorms tomorrow. I'm wondering if you would not like to join us and take a look around."

She looked at Grace—the Lycan Queen—what was she supposed to say? Was it an invitation or an order? The day had just been too much—too many emotions, too much to consider and then she had to worry about her brother.

"There are also a few humans I need to interview and I think I could most certainly use your help. It's going to be a very touchy subject and you're so good with people. You seem to set others at ease and that would be invaluable as I explain what they've gotten themselves into."

Xander, Grace's half-brother and the pack's tech guy, shot out of his chair, face red and eyes blazing with fury.

"You're exposing us to the humans?"

Wrenching her fingers as she watched Grace flash her violet eyes at her younger half-brother—a sign of her authority. Xander reclaimed his seat but glared back. "That's a violation of our laws."

"The Fae have already pre-screened the individuals who are…shall we say…more open to the idea of our kind. And if they become a problem, the Fae will just use their gifts to erase their memory." Grace kept her voice calm, though her clenched jaw demonstrated her frustration with Xander.

Wendy knew there had been tension between the siblings before, but they seemed to have come to a better place, though Xander still challenged Grace quite frequently.

"Did you do something different with your hair?" Colin asked waving his fork at her, swirling it around.

Every muscle tensed. Was this going to be when he mentioned seeing her running with Zoltar? Was he going to out her at dinner? The question startled Wendy. It apparently threw everyone else for a loop too as all eyes were on her.

"Interested in becoming a cosmetologist?" Roman teased, tossing a roll at him. He sat stiff, allowing it to bounce off his chest.

Colin studied her, pulling his brows together while waving his finger, encircling her. "You look different."

She shot a glance at Zoltar, who was smiling back. *Did he really turn back my clock?* She had to get some control back of the situation. "Grace, I'd be happy to check out the new building with you and help with the interviews. Thank you for the invitation." She scooted her chair back. "If you'll excuse me." She *had* to get to a mirror.

Fast as she could, she hustled up the stairs to her room, stopping at the mirror. "Holy hell!" Every gray hair was gone. Every worry line, erased. One kiss made her look like a woman in her early thirties, instead of one pushing mid-forties or 200 in the case of a Lycan. One kiss from Zoltar had turned back the clock, which seemed to run fast for her.

"Wendy?" Nala stood behind her with her hands folded. "Is everything okay?"

The Alpha was good at sneaking up, a skill which would suit her well. Wendy stood a little straighter. "I'm fine. Thank you."

Nala cleared her throat and lifted her chin a bit higher. "You know, uh, Colin is very worried that he's hurt your feelings. He's been stewing about it all day."

"He has?" Wendy hadn't known Colin to worry much about her. True, when he was Alpha, he worried a lot, but it never seemed to be aimed at her. Maybe because she'd always taken care of him, she hadn't noticed.

*

"You're really exposing us to humans?" Xander prodded as he pounded the handle of his fork against the oak table.

Grace crossed her arms across her chest. Her left brow shot up toward her hair line. "Just how many Supernaturals can you find with the qualifications to become a professor at an accredited university?"

"Three," he groaned. His shoulders slumped forward, apparently losing his battle with the Lycan Queen.

"Exactly. We don't have time to wait, so we have to go with human professors for now. Don't worry, little brother, we're taking every precaution. I think having humans around will help us blend better into society. "

Colin put his hand on Zoltar's shoulder. "Thank you for suggesting Wendy for the university. I really think she's a good fit and if she can let go of this place, I'm sure she'll be happy there."

Zoltar forced his lips into a smile, eager to get the Lycan's dangerous hand off his shoulder. "I'm certain she will be fine. She seems like a strong woman, your sister. I also noticed how organized she was with the large group we had here with no notice. Those kinds of skills will serve the students well."

Releasing his grip, Colin leaned in on his elbows. "She needs a purpose. She's spent far too long taking care of everyone else. It's her time to have something that's...hers." His mouth turned down in a frown. His brow furrowed as he stared at his plate.

Was the frown caused by seeing his sister running with a Centaur? He focused in on Colin, searching his thoughts. *"She deserves a mate, happiness, and a family. I've been so selfish."* The Lycan seemed pure of heart, making him feel more at ease.

"Don't worry. This university equates to a brighter future for us all, your sister included. I'm sure she'll find what she's looking for there." He stood from his chair. "Thank you for an excellent meal, but I'm going to retire for the evening." He made his way to the guest room and locked the door behind him.

There was something about this woman that pulled at him. He had premonitions about her after first meeting her, but his visions were always a little fuzzy. He saw them by a fire drinking wine. Because his premonitions were sporadic and unclear, they could mean anything. It didn't *necessarily* mean they were meant to be together. She roused him though. She roused him in a way he'd never experienced. He wanted to be near her, to feel the warmth coming from her. He found himself reveling in her smile and pained by anything less.

For far too long, his kind spent their lives alone, unmated because there were no women in their species. Women of other species didn't want to be outcasts of their packs and marry the enemy. This new beginning could mean actual love instead of lust for the Centaurs. He had high hopes for his herd.

He scooped up a book on Lycan bonding, devouring

each word, determined to learn more. True, honest-to-goodness, reliable literature on Lycanthropy was difficult to find. There was too much fiction and mythology blended into most reference books he could get his hands on. He traced the author of this particular Lycanthropy guide. A Lycan scholar, long since dead, had managed to get it published prior to his demise.

This woman stirred desire in him he'd not felt in his two hundred years. Thoughts of her swelled his cock to an unprecedented hardness. He stood from the bed and dropped his pants to the floor. He imagined their bodies intertwined, Wendy's warmth enveloping him as he eased into her, while their lips danced in a lover's kiss.

Hoping for release, he stroked his hard-on. He licked his lips, remembering the sweetness of hers gracing his in the woods, how she melted into him. He wanted to put her back against a tree and take her there. Picturing her delicious plump lips wrapped around his cock, he gave his balls a firm squeeze. That image was all he needed for his release to come.

Wendy wrecked him. She had to be his. He only hoped she would accept him.

*

Wendy crawled under the covers. *So Z wasn't tricking me. His kiss actually had an effect on me. Well, more than making my knees buckle. What would a Centaur King want with me? I'm just an average Lycan—nothing special.*

Continuing to question herself and Zoltar's motives, she turned on her side and stared at her pillow, her stomach doing flops. *Centaur sex is supposed to be phenomenal. I haven't had sex in two decades. Do I even remember how?*

She groaned as lust reverberated through her body once more. The stupid Centaur had twisted up her mind and body. She needed to focus on what she was going to do about moving. Would she go to the university and be the Headmistress? What did being a Headmistress even mean? Was she qualified?

There were too many questions in her head. She needed rest, but she couldn't stop her mind from pictured him standing in the woods, his jeans barely clinging on at the hip. How easy it would be to slip them off and explore his nether regions. *Stop it! Knock it off, dammit!* She cursed herself, burying her face in her pillow.

"He is part Lycan. He could be our mate." Her wolf, who was usually quiet, spoke to her.

"Fat chance."

"Our world is changing. It might be more acceptable now. Consider it."

Consider it? She was damned near panting at one simple kiss. She turned to mush and couldn't think straight around him. That's not the mark of a good mating. How would their life be?

"What am I thinking? He doesn't want any more than a Centaur baby to cart off to his pack." A tear rolled down her cheek. She just wanted a mate and pups like any other Lycan. Why was she doomed to be alone?

Wendy wasn't in the habit of wallowing in self-pity. It irked her that she sobbed into her pillow, mourning the love that never came. He'd showed an interest, true. But what sort of future could a blended couple have? Centaurs and Lycans didn't mate. They didn't bond. Centaurs came in, seduced and impregnated them for years, only to leave a grieving, childless mother full of shame. She wasn't going to be just another mark in his belt. An incubator, she was not!

THREE

Wendy watched the others scurry around after breakfast, getting ready for their day. She was dressed in her favorite black jeans and red knit sweater. Colin had bought her a pair of black boots that were comfortable, which she'd chosen since she could only assume would be appropriate for the amount of walking they'd have to do. But she worried she was underdressed for the meetings Grace had asked her to attend.

To her relief, she didn't have to wait long. The royal couple descended the stairs, both in jeans.

"Good, you're ready." Grace gave her a quick hug.

"Z is already waiting at the car," Roman said as he kissed her forehead.

"Z?"

Grace rolled her eyes. "There's plenty of room. I drive a four door. Come on, we don't want to run behind."

She flung her bag over her shoulder. "After you." The last thing she needed was more time with the Centaur. Knowing she should be thankful for the age-lift, she couldn't help but feel he would be a detriment to any romantic future might be in store. He was a *Centaur*. She

17

didn't need seduction—not now, not when she was trying to make a life altering decision.

They found him leaning against the front passenger side of the car. "Are Lycans always this slow?" He smiled at Roman and gave Grace a playful wink.

"Lycan women, yes."

Grace smacked Roman in the arm. "We are right on time! Get in the car."

She was uncomfortable with the simple fact the royal couple would be in the front, leaving her with Zoltar in the back seat, sitting side by side. She wanted to keep her distance—a safe distance from his hormones and sexual prowess. He only added insult to injury when he held the door open for her.

"Thank you," she forced out. Why was a simple act of chivalry so offensive? Ducking in the car, she grabbed the door and swung it shut, wishing he'd stay outside the car and not climb in, mere inches from her.

When he sat next to her and closed his door, his smell invaded her senses. After years of preparing meals and baking, she didn't have a hard time picking spices out by smell. He smelled like a distinct mix of cinnamon, cardamom, vanilla and that manly musk. The scent that made women face-plant in their man's used t-shirt. *Dammit. I don't know if I want to dunk him in milk or strip him naked.*

She stared out the window quietly, watching the earth move by at a quick pace.

"So Roman and I will show you around the university." Grace said as she stared at her in the rearview. "Z will show you around the residence wing while Roman and I take care of some business."

Wendy looked at Zoltar. "Great."

He smiled back at her and raised one brow. "It'll be better than our stroll in the woods."

Grace and Roman shot glances at each other and Wendy did not miss Roman's smirk.

"Nice to see you set the bar low. Keeps your success rate high, at least." She tried to hide her smile as she resumed staring out the window of the car.

"Did you talk to her about teaching the Lycanthropy class yet?" he leaned up toward the front seat, looking at Roman.

"Nope. We don't even know if she wants the job."

"I'm right here, you know." Wendy tossed her hands up and let them fall to her lap. "What's this about teaching?" She cleared her throat. "I don't have a college education."

Grace looked at her in the rearview. "Well, Xander is going to resolve the little certificate issue, but honestly, it won't be a sanctioned class as far as the state is concerned. But I can't think of anyone better to teach a class on Lycans."

"What on earth makes you say that?" She clutched her purse, looking for comfort. Why was everyone making deductions about her? She didn't like being the topic of conversation. Her chest ached as she wished she'd have stayed with the pack instead of agreeing to the field trip.

"Well, you've been reading about our kind for three quarters of a century. I have one final book for you to read, courtesy of the vampires, and then you'll know everything there is. All you have to do is pass that knowledge onto the kids. We're already having books printed up on the matter. You can create your own syllabus. Really, guys. I wanted to talk to her about this when I had material to show her. Thanks for fucking it up." She squeezed Roman's thigh.

"I'm teaching the Mythological Creatures class as well as Combat Tactics." Zoltar said with a smile, leaning slightly toward her. His bronze skin set off his pearly white teeth. "Perhaps we can swap techniques? Old war stories, perhaps?"

She sucked in a breath of air and held it. She'd cooked, cleaned, and organized events. What on earth made these crazy people think she could teach?

"Because," Grace said into the mirror, "you have been teaching for years. You just don't realize it."

Roman turned in his seat to face her and wiggled his brows. "Neat ability our Queen has, isn't it?"

"I've learned to turn it off and not invade the privacy of others, but she's practically screaming back there." Grace continued to monitor her through the rearview as if she were a child about to smack a sibling.

She sank down in her seat, with nowhere to retreat. *One step at a time. Fuck the Gods, she heard my thought about dipping Z in milk!*

Grace led out a snicker. "Sorry, Wendy. I'm really sorry. Quiet your thoughts a bit and I shouldn't hear them." She giggled again. When Roman looked at her she only shook her head. "Not in a million years, pal. Stay out of my head."

She recited poetry in her head, then lyrics to her favorite songs…anything, really, to keep from embarrassing herself again. She breathed a sigh of relief when they finally made it to the university and out of the car.

The building was massive, built like an old castle. To the West, she could see the Centaurs, in their true form, hauling wagons of bricks and stone, raising walls and pouring concrete. The Dwarves were assisting with the masonry, from what she could see.

"If you would have told me two short years ago that Centaurs and Dwarves would be working side-by-side, I would have sworn you were drunk." She shook her head.

Zoltar leaned over and whispered in her ear. "Would you like to be more astonished? Look over there." He pointed off to the East wing where Fae and Pixies were on the Centaurs backs. "Not in my lifetime have we ever given anyone a lift. Never. This is real progress, Wendy, something for which we should all feel an immense amount of pride."

"I could not have said it better myself, Z." Roman slapped him on the shoulder. "It's nice to have peace."

She looked around, trying to let her brain register everything her eye could see. Zoltar looped his arm in hers. "You don't want to miss this part." She didn't fight him. With someone to hold on to, maybe she wouldn't run into a pillar or something while she was distracted, gazing at the sights.

The entry was grand, five stories tall, turret style with a winding staircase that looked like it was carved into the stone.

"The Fae assisted us in finding wood from trees that were already deceased, so we didn't harm Mother Nature. The Pixies worked a little magic twisting and braiding the thick wooden vines to make the hand rails. The Gnomes have been fantastic about running wires for us. It's as if they finally feel like their tiny size was of some use." Zoltar pointed to different features as he spoke. "This is the biggest collaboration in all of our history. Isn't it something?"

"What? Oh, yes. Yes, it's marvelous. I really can't take it all in fast enough."

He squeezed her arm.

"Let's show her some of the classes," Grace waved toward a set of stairs. "First, when I was in college, it was absolutely frustrating how one class would be on one side of the campus, and then my next class was on the other side. So, if you choose to take the position, you'll get a map so you can make workable schedules for the staff as well as the students." She cleared her throat. "That's where your fantastic organizational skills come in."

She could only nod and follow, holding onto Zoltar in case she tripped. The tour of the class rooms went so fast she could hardly retain the image of their grandeur before Grace and Roman left her with Zoltar.

"It's so beautiful."

"I agree."

She looked up at him. "I can't believe how quickly this all came together." Astonishment at the magnificence and grandeur of the school left her dumbfounded and amazed.

"Thank you. I worked tirelessly on the plans."

She released his arm and stepped back. "*You* did this?"

He shrugged. "It's my design. Most of the stone was reclaimed from the building that used to house your High Council. The wood was brought by the Fae, as I said. The labor has been accomplished through volunteers."

"Amazing. You...your design is amazing." Her jaw hung open.

He smiled. "I'm amazing. I'll remember you said that." He winked before spinning on his heel. "Follow me. It's time for you to see what will make this a home for many."

She jogged ahead to catch up with him. "When do we open?"

"We?" He looked down at her and raised a brow. "Does this mean you want to be part of this?"

Placing her palm on her forehead, she grimaced. "I admit, yesterday, I was shocked and confused but how could I look at all of this and walk away? This is amazing."

Instead of saying anything, he looked ahead and smiled. He held out his arm for her to take.

She looped her arm in his, eager for more of the tour.

"The East wing houses the classes, as you just saw. The West wing is all about living. Down this hall will be the boys' dorm." He turned the corner and stepped through a door sized arch way which led to stairs and more halls. "The Dwarves will carve hall and room numbers to help our students find their way." He opened the first door. A small kitchenette rested on the left side of the room. In the rear of the apartment was a dining table. Her eyes naturally scanned to the right, where there was a sitting area.

"Four students per room when we're full. There's one bathroom per dorm room, so there will be no communal showers. Grace was fairly insistent about this. She wants it to feel more like a home. This is the students' sleeping quarters." He opened up the final door to a bedroom with two bunk beds, four small closet doors and four small bureaus for clothes.

"This is wonderful. It's like a small apartment rather than an actual college dorm. Tiffany sent me some pictures of her dorm and I have to tell you, it's really not fit for a Lycan. I can only assume it wouldn't be fit for any shifter. It's so tiny and cramped." She shook her head. "But this is nice. It feels...like a home."

He smiled and nodded, his blond locks waving. "Your endorsement is music to my ears. I really worried about the setup. It pleased your Queen, but it coming from you is really something."

Since when is her opinion more valuable than the Queen's?

"Now to the Professor's living space. How are your feet?" he asked, looking down at the thin soles on her boots.

With a glance at her sore feet, she shrugged. "A little tired. We've been walking for a few hours."

The air around him shimmered. His head and shoulders began to rise in the air as he shifted into Centaur. "Hop on."

She shook her head. "No, I couldn't."

Extending his hand to her, he tilted his head. "Please. With these hooves, the floor doesn't make my feet so tired. Stone is hard on the ankle and foot."

The sound of her heart thundered in her ears as her heart beat quickened. The boots weren't offering her the comfort they normally did. Her feet ached, but mounting Zoltar wasn't the ideal situation.

"Please, allow me to take you to the next location and give your feet a rest."

Her hand shook as she put it in his. He pulled hard, heaving her onto his back. The instant relief to her feet was welcomed but Wendy had a new problem. Her legs were now wrapped around his horse body and the heat from him was seeping through her pants. It made her mind run wild.

After clearing her throat, she asked, "How far is it?"

He turned his head to the side. "I can't really run on these floors, or I'd have you there in less than a minute. But at this pace, five minutes, maybe a few more."

She cursed herself for not shifting into wolf form and just padding along, though cold stone on her paws wouldn't feel much better than her humanoid feet in boots. She kept quiet. The only sound was that of Zoltar's hooves clacking down the stone hall. She tried not to watch the muscles of his shoulders ripple as he walked. She tried not to smell his unique aroma which seemed to be everywhere. She really struggled not to grab hold of his blonde locks.

"Here we are." He held out his hand to help her off, but Wendy had already dismounted before he could give her any assistance. Swiftly, he shifted back to human form before opening the first door. "Much like the dorms, each hall leads to separate living spaces and the stairs go up to the floors above."

When he pushed the door open, she gasped. The floors were hardwood with large area rugs of plush carpeting throughout. The kitchen held cherry wood cabinets and granite countertops. A decent sized stainless steel fridge and stove nestled in as if they were made specifically for that kitchen. She ran her fingers along the granite countertop as she made her way to the small dining area.

"Since there aren't four people in these units, the dining area is quaint, but the living area is a bit more spacious." He slid his fingers from her elbow to her wrist. "This way."

Despite the warmth where he touched her causing her to shiver, she allowed him to lead her into the living room, which was spacious, yet cozy. It had yet to be furnished, but she could already picture where she would put the couch, chair, and tables.

"Each living space will be equipped with a television and cable. Your Queen seems to think it's important for us to get acquainted with human news and pop culture to blend in better with the rest of the world." He shook his head. "I disagree, but I seem to be in the minority."

"Look at this built-in book case!" She said, not caring about the television. "The woodwork is extraordinary!" She ran her hands along the carved wood.

"You'll love the bedroom, then. Come along." He waved for her to follow.

As she admired the view of his ass, she trailed behind him to the bedroom where a carved bedframe resided. "It can be slid together to accommodate a queen, but right now it's set up for a king." He cleared his throat. "The closet over here—was made with women in mind. Storage bins for shoes and things and plenty of room for clothing."

Brushing his arm as she passed, she headed to the bathroom. "Wow. I can imagine soaking in that tub." She smiled at the bear claw bathtub. "That would be so lovely."

A deep throaty chuckle escaped his lips. "Each unit is set up the same. The resident gets to choose the drapes and furniture from a catalog we have from a wholesaler with whom we have a financial arrangement." He leaned against the door frame. "Because we want it to feel like a home, not a temporary residence."

"I'm speechless." She found a tremendous amount of respect for Zoltar—the fact that the plans for every feature were his. The forethought of making others comfortable was the most predominant aspect which caught her off guard.

"Oh, one other thing, your Xander has installed something called Wee-Fee in the building. There isn't one point you won't have it." He scratched his head. "I think."

She laughed. "Wee-Fee?" She put her hands on her knees to brace herself.

He joined her, even though whatever tickled her was clearly at his expense. "Did I say something funny?"

"It's not 'Wee-Fee', it's Wi-Fi. It's wireless internet." She wiped her eyes with the back of her hand. "I'm sorry for laughing like that. It really wasn't *that* funny."

"You have a lovely laugh, Wendy. Please don't apologize." He pushed off the door frame. "We'd better get you to the admin offices for your meetings."

"Thank you for showing me around, Z. The building is magnificent." She followed him out of the unit, closing the door behind her. Her cheeks were beginning to ache, making her realize the amount of time she'd been smiling. It had been a long time since she'd experienced that sensation. She wondered if it were the magnificence of the building, or the company she was keeping.

"The pleasure of your company is thanks enough."

She wanted to say something, but words evaded her. He complimented her continuously. She looked at him as they strolled down a long corridor. "So that kiss," she said, praying her face wouldn't turn red for the millionth time, "you weren't as full of shit as I thought you were. The grays are gone as are the lines. Want to tell me what that was about?"

He shrugged. "I told you I was a bit of a healer."

"That would insinuate I was sick, in need of healing. Am I sick?" *And how would he know?*

"Goddess, no. You're not ill, Wendy. But love does something for our kind. Love actually does something for humans, as I understand it, as well. But from what I can see, you've spent your time giving every ounce of yourself to others, and not getting much in return. It was aging you prematurely. You're not receiving the same positive energy back that say...a mate, or children might give."

The familiar black haze of loneliness invaded her chest once again. "Yeah," she croaked. "But at my age, I don't see that changing."

He glanced down at her, but only for a split second.

"Perhaps."

FOUR

Zoltar left her with Grace and a waiting room full of potential professors. He could feel the females staring at him. He focused on his androstenol production, trying to calm the female-attracting scent his body naturally threw off.

He knew what this meant for him and rushed to find a private area. The moment he thought he was alone, he let the tears flow. Controlling androgens or androstenol usually meant an increased production in progesterone, the female hormone. He'd been fighting to keep his natural scent at bay while with Wendy. If he were going to win her heart, he didn't want it to be because of his high output of androstenol, the sex pheromone.

He slid down the wall, resting on the floor, and cried.

"What in tarnation?" A male voice startled him. He ceased focusing on his hormone control and rose to his feet. The Dwarf staring at him combed his red beard with his stubby hands. "What's with you Centaurs and the darned cryin'?"

He lifted his chin. "It takes a lot out of us to keep our hormone production in check, so as not to seduce your women. We swore an oath to all of you and we intend to keep it. This is a sad byproduct of that effort." He wiped his tears on the back of his hand.

The Dwarf threw his hands in the air. "Shoot! Go get a blow job from a Pixie. They don't seem to mind, little whores."

He crossed his arms over his chest. "That's no way to talk about them, sir. Remember our goal is to accept each other, to live in peace and harmony. Shaming the Pixies for being sexual creatures is rude."

"Well then quit yer damn cryin' son. We got work to do!" The Dwarf waddled away cursing. "Fuckin' giant-ass Centaurs, cryin' all over the damned place. Warriors my ass! Nothin' but big ass hooved sissies if you ask me!"

He couldn't help but chuckle at being called a big ass hooved sissy. Apparently, he wasn't the only Centaur suffering from keeping their sexuality at bay. Perhaps it was time to check on his people. He shifted into his true form and made his way out of the building. Once outside, he stretched his legs as he galloped to the far West wing where construction was still underway.

"Where is Grog?" he asked as he approached.

Theron, Zoltar's beta shrugged. "Two dozen of our men are in the woods, trying to retain some control." It was worse than he thought.

"How are you holding up?"

Theron cracked his neck. "I'm hanging on. We swore an oath."

"That shouldn't mean we torture ourselves like this. Let me see what I can do." He whistled and waited for his team to assemble. When they all circled him, he pounded his chest. "Release your control."

He saw them all sigh in relief as they released the control they had on themselves. He noticed a group of Pixies gathering behind them, ogling. "Now, we run. On my lead." He tore off toward the forest, with his herd on his rear. He led them through five laps of the three-hundred acre property.

Ella, the Pixie Queen and Roman, the Lycan King, were waiting for them when they returned to the jobsite.

"What is going on?" Roman asked. His brow was furrowed and his eyes darted around to the many centaurs surrounding him.

He gulped in a large breath of air. "Let's find a private place to converse." He led them toward the forest, away from the workers. "My herd is struggling. We swore an oath when we arrived, so all of the other species would relax around us. For us, that meant controlling our natural excretion of sex hormone. It takes a lot of focus and control, on top of the physical labor. We are intent on keeping our oath, but…"

"You're suffering?" Ella's eyes widened with realization.

"In a matter of speaking, yes. Otherwise fierce warriors are reduced to tears as our chemistry becomes off balance." He was keeping the fact about the female hormones to himself.

With her arms crossed over her chest, she studied him. Her spiky black hair glistened in the sun like oil. "Are you controlling yours right now?"

He nodded.

"Stop for a moment. I'm curious to see how powerful it is."

With a glance at Roman, he shook his head. "I'm not sure that's a grand idea."

The Lycan King shrugged. "She asked for it, man."

He relinquished control.

The Pixie's eyes shot open wide. "Holy fucking hell. That's powerful."

Roman sniffed the air and shrugged, "Guess it doesn't work on me."

She glanced around. "You have one Dwarf female working here, among a group of my people. I can send the women to the other side of the grounds and ask the Dwarf to tag along. You could work during the day without controlling yourselves. Would that help?"

"Very much." He nodded in agreement. Several hours of relief a day would go a long way to keep them from completely breaking down.

With a leer, she looked at Roman. "My people are sexual creatures by nature. Perhaps we could allow some leeway."

He shrugged and looked away. "That's between you two. You *do* have cool contraception at your disposal."

Zoltar had no idea what Roman was referring to.

"Such an arrangement would give some relief to my men. They could let go of the control during the day and seek some companionship in the evening. But only if your kind agree."

"You mean the women?" Roman asked.

Ella shifted on her feet. "No, Roman. Pixie men are sexual beings too." She glanced at Zoltar. "We have an agreement." She stuck out her hand and shook his, sealing the deal.

"My men will keep this contained to non-working hours. We're nearing completion and my goal is to reduce the distractions, not add to them."

She gave one strong and firm nod. "Agreed."

Roman rubbed his forehead. "This is the oddest business arrangement I've ever witnessed. I'm going back inside the school where it's sane." He shifted to wolf form and ran toward the main entrance.

She glanced down at his cock. "Are you in need of some company this evening?"

Shaking his head, he held his hands up, palms facing her. "No thank you." He pointed over his shoulder at Theron. "My beta, however, has been known to be quite skillful. I'm sure you'd be pleased with his performance."

Her red blood red lips spread into a wide grin. "Most excellent. Let's make this announcement over dinner." She turned on her heel and sauntered back toward the building.

He looked up at the tower. Wendy was up there somewhere. He hadn't wanted to take Ella up on her offer and taint a possible relationship with a mate by soiling himself with meaningless sex. He had sex with a Pixie before. It had been the most orgasms he'd ever had in one evening. None of that mattered if it wasn't with the woman he was sure he loved. He'd settle for one orgasm a year if it meant it was with someone special.

"Something wrong with the building, bro?" Theron asked nudging him.

"What?" He shook his head. "No. Just deep in thought. Listen, I've made an arrangement for our men. We'll discuss this at dinner." He looked at his watch. "Which is in an hour. Where the hell did the day go? Anyway, I daresay everyone's spirits are due to be lifted."

Theron nodded and left Zoltar gazing at the building.

*

"You understand," Grace said, "that what you've learned here is not to be shared with any other human?"

The woman sitting across from Grace's desk nodded. "I always knew. Somehow, I always knew."

Wendy looked at the older human woman, whose gray hair was wound in a bun. "Young shifters are quite hot-headed, especially the males. You'll have to rule with an iron fist. You understand that? They'll naturally take orders from you. It's in our nature to follow the hierarchy. So when they start to get out of hand, you need to bark orders at them. Can you handle that at your age?"

The woman laughed. "I raised five sons. And while they might have been human, they were anything but docile. I can assure you."

A smile spread across Wendy's lips as she looked at Grace. "I like her."

Grace stood from her chair. "Then welcome, Mrs. Rutger. You are our new English-Lit Professor. My assistant will give you the hiring packet as you leave. Someone will lead you to the residence so you can get a feel for what you'll need to order for your home. We'll see you soon."

"Thank you. I'm looking forward to it." She stood from her chair. "Ms. Baker, I look forward to our friendship. I like your tenacity."

After the woman left the room, Grace leaned back in her chair. "The next one is going to be a doozy. It's my friend Barb from college. She has no idea I'm a Lycan, but when I called to tell her about the position and that it was unusual, she seemed eager."

She tried to hide the shock she felt. "Maybe it's better if I do the shifting this time. My wolf is half the size." A Lycan might be difficult for a human to accept, but Grace's Lycan was enormous due to her royal blood.

Grace chuckled. "That's probably a good idea." She leaned in and pressed the intercom. "Send in the next candidate."

"It'll be fine, Grace. I can feel your anxiety. If she doesn't take it well, we'll have the Fae erase her memory and you two will still be friends." She gave Grace's shoulder a squeeze.

"It's not just that. I was an entirely different woman last time Barb saw me. I didn't even know I was a Lycan, let alone this." She motioned over her body.

"Oh my God!" The woman squealed as she bolted through the door. "Grace! You look wonderful! What the hell...you're married?" She looked at the simple gold band on Grace's finger.

Grace held up her hands. "I know. I know. I'm the world's worst friend. We can get caught up on the personal side of things after the meeting. Wendy doesn't need to be here for that."

She stood and extended her hand. "Wendy Baker. Nice to meet you, Barbara."

Barb shook her hand and gave her a once over.

She felt something odd with this woman. Her hand felt warm, unlike the other human hands she was forced to shake today. There was a different energy about her...and a smell, not a human smell.

"Grace," she began. How was she going to warn her?

Grace paid no mind to her. "I'm afraid there is a small thirty second test you have to pass before we can begin the interview. Are you game?"

"Am I ever? Bring it on!" She cracked her neck. "Ju-jitsu? Hand to hand? Got some asshole you want me to take out?"

The Queen laughed. "No. Just a test to see how open minded you are. Are you ready?"

When Barb nodded, Grace looked at Wendy. "You're up."

She smiled at Barb. "Try not to be startled. This can shock most people. Okay?"

The woman tossed her head back and laughed. "I've been living in California. You can't shock me anymore. Let's get on with it."

She stood, the air around her shimmered as she took her time shifting into wolf.

"God damn it Grace! I fuckin' knew it!" She shot out of her chair. "I knew it!"

Wendy shifted back and moved in front of Grace as her protective instincts took over. "Let's remain calm."

Grace placed her palm on her arm and gently moved her out of the way. "What do you mean, you knew? You're not freaked out by this?"

Barb threw her hands in the air. "Of course not."

"You knew? How?"

Wendy watched her Queen, studying the woman across the desk. Grace didn't appear alarmed, only curious. The woman seemed excited, but not angry. She waited at the ready to protect her Queen.

"I would always start to think I smelled it on you. Then your Gran would say you were having a diabetic thing, shoot you with that stuff, and then I couldn't smell it anymore."

"Smell it?" Grace's jaw fell slack. "You mean?"

"Shit. You didn't know…of course you didn't." The woman stood then quite quickly shifted into a panther before shifting back. "I'm a shifter."

"She's not human," Wendy uttered. "I felt something. I tried to warn you."

Grace jumped up, ran around the desk, and threw her arms around the werepanther-woman. "God! Barb! No wonder we were so close."

Wendy stepped back to give the women some space. They were friends, after all. She went to the window and gazed toward the West wing. Zoltar was there, talking with Roman and Ella. *Damn, even with half a horse body he's sexy as hell.* But why the meeting? What was going on? Roman shifted to wolf and ran toward the building. Ella stayed behind, close to Zoltar.

Her chest blazed hot. *Stay away from him you fuckin' Pixie!*

Zoltar pointed toward another Centaur, and the Pixie's gaze followed. *Get your own, Centaur, lady. Wait? What the hell am I thinking? What's wrong with me?*

Z looked right at her. He looked right where she stood in the window. *Yeah, I see you. You son-of-a-bitch!*

"Wendy?" Grace said. "I've called your name three times."

"I still can't believe you're mated with that hotty from the bar. Way to go, girl." Barb said shaking her head.

She shook her head. "I'm sorry, Grace. I was trying to give you two some private time."

Grace gave her a soft smile and followed it up with a wink. "Well, at least I know you weren't eaves dropping. Now, help me fill her in."

Wendy addressed Barb, going over her duties as a professor. "Obviously, you know how young shifters can be."

"Pains in the ass. Don't worry. I got this."

She scanned the woman's resume. "If you don't mind me asking, why the change in employment?"

Barb shook her head. "If you can believe it, I hate being a fucking lawyer with every fiber of my being." She leaned back. "I didn't think far enough ahead. I wanted the job, the power and prestige, but honestly, a shifter stuck in an office twelve hours a day, then dinner parties and shit at night. Stupid."

"Well, Grace you can cover it from here." She gathered her purse, tossing it over her shoulder.

Grace looked at the clock. "Yes, let's go down to dinner. It should be served any time now." She looped her arm around the shoulder of her friend. "Let me show you the mess hall. It's fantastic."

Wendy trailed behind, lost in thought. She surveyed her personal situation with the move. She didn't own much beyond her own clothes and some books. She'd never wanted for anything either. She had a driver's license but never owned a car. She drove Colin's car, then Michelle's after she died. But she rarely drove. Her furniture wasn't much either. It would be easy, logistically, for her to move.

How hard would it be to adjust without the pack she'd had all of her life? Would she be able to make a pack here at the school? She knew Roman and Grace. Would that be enough?

She froze in her tracks when they reached the dining area. It was as grand as the rest of the grounds with long hand carved banquet tables, silver candelabras adorning the walls and each table, beautiful masonry everywhere and natural marble embedded throughout.

"The Dwarves masonry work is amazing, is it not?" Grace nudged her.

"This whole building is amazing. I feel like I'm in a palace, and horribly underdressed."

Grace snickered and tucked her brown hair behind her ear. "Well, the workers are dressed pretty casually, so I think we're fine. Of course, once school starts, it'll be business casual attire for us. Come. Sit. They're about to serve soon." She pulled her to a table where they both took a seat. Once Barb sat next to Grace, they went back to chattering, allowing her mind to wander.

The workers started filling in. From the looks of it, they'd done the best to clean themselves up after a long, hard day. While they looked beat, they were all in clean clothes looking freshly showered.

"Mind if I sit?" Zoltar had his hand on the chair next to her.

"It's a free world." She waved him off.

He released the chair and stood stiff. "I don't want to bother you." He walked ten paces away and took a seat at another table.

Her shoulders shrunk. He was being polite, and she'd been rude. Her mother would have tanned her backside for such behavior. She should know better. To top it off, he was a King and she treated him like something lower than average by dismissing him.

Roman entered the dining hall and stood at the front. When everyone took their seats, he called for their attention. "Something has been brought to our attention. As many of you know, the Centaurs were aware when they made their presence known to us, that there would be some tension due to the history we all share. They've taken great measures to ensure their oath to us and maintain the trust they're working so hard to build."

He ran his fingers through his hair, scratching at the back of his head. She knew this to be a sign of stress in Roman, and instantly started to worry.

"What we didn't know was the physical and psychological pain they would have to endure to maintain their oath. As Zoltar has explained it, they excrete an exceptionally high amount of a certain hormone that attracts females. They've learned to control this hormone, but not without consequence to their physical and emotional states."

There were mumbles among the women, some grousing, some looking hopeful. She turned to look at Zoltar, who kept a firm eye on Roman. *Pain?*

"Therefore, during working hours, only males will work on the West wing. This will allow them to release the control they have on themselves throughout most of the day. We don't want our brothers to suffer and this seems like a logical solution to a complicated problem. Now, for a more complex situation, the Pixies have means of copulating without conception that's highly effective and Ella has granted permission for her kind to, uh, assist with the needs of some of the Centaurs' needs. As we move to a more peaceful time, we need to make adjustments as needed. It isn't our wish to micromanage your lives. It is our position that you all are individuals with needs and desires. Do as you wish. For those of you with concerns please know Zoltar has given his word, his men will not join with any mated female without her partner's consent. Now that I've given you plenty to discuss over dinner, let's eat."

He took three giant steps until he was sitting across from Grace. "Well that was uncomfortable."

"What sort of pain are they in?" Wendy felt her face burn with embarrassment as the question crossed her lips.

He sighed. "A lot of emotional suffering from what I gather. Playing around with hormones doesn't come without repercussion. From what I understand, they've all been keeping a tight wrap on things since approaching us at our wedding. They're starting to have breakdowns."

She fidgeted with the napkin in front of her then slowly scooted her chair back, stood and walked over to Zoltar. "Excuse me," she said as she placed her hand on his shoulder.

"Wendy?" He looked up at her, his eyes wide.

"I think I owe you an apology. Would you please join us at our table?" She didn't care that her face burned red with embarrassment this time. It was small penance for being so rude.

He nodded and followed her. "What made you change your mind?" he asked as he sat.

"I was rude. It was uncalled for. I wanted to say something at the time, but Roman came in and started making the announcement." She shook her head. "It delayed me for a few."

Gazing down toward the table, his brows pulled together. "I was beginning to worry I had offended you."

Her heart sank. Here she was brooding over being lonely and this man...this man was so nice and she had been less than nice.

"So am I forgiven?"

He smiled at her. "Nothing to forgive."

Trays of food were served, giving her a much needed distraction. When the lid was lifted on her plate, her mouth watered. A porterhouse steak, a baked sweet potato and sautéed green beans glistened on the plate. Now she had to figure out how to devour this meal without looking like a pig. She cut a slice of meat and took a bite. "Wow, this is fantastic."

From across the table Roman waved his fork in a circle. "We have some of the best cooks we could find. Of course the students won't be eating like this but with so much work going on, we need our workers strong and healthy. A good hot meal at the end of the day makes a huge difference." He smiled as he crammed a huge chunk of steak in his mouth. "Plus men like steak."

"Men? Women like steak!" She cut off a big hunk of her own and shoved it in her mouth. "Pup."

With a roll of the eyes, he chuckled. She'd always thought of him like a little brother. He and Colin had been so close it was hard to think of him as anything less.

"Z, I know I've said it a million times already. But you have really done something special here. The building is fantastic." She nudged him. "You're quite the engineer."

Thick lips curved into a smile that he attempted to hide

as he wiped his mouth with the napkin. "I'll take all of the compliments you can dish out." He folded his napkin neatly before placing it on his plate. "The meal was fantastic, Roman. Good choice on those cooks! I haven't had a steak cooked this perfectly in ages."

There was pride in the smile Roman returned to him.

Zoltar leaned over toward her. "If I can push just a little, I was wondering if you'd honor me with your company. I'd like to share a glass of wine with you and a chat, if that's okay with you?"

She opened her mouth to object.

He interrupted before she could speak. "I promise to stay as honorable as I have all day."

Snapping her mouth shut before she could object and offend him again, she let a smile spread across her lips instead before simply replying, "Okay."

He led her out of the dining hall and down another corridor. "I already have my living space set up. I've been staying here for the last few weeks. This way, you get some insight to how your space will look with some furniture." He glanced at her while they walked.

"I'd very much like to know about this pain Roman discussed."

He chuckled. "I'm not a colt anymore, Wendy. I'm fine."

She didn't buy it. Roman would have specified if it were only the young Centaurs who were suffering. On the other hand, she had suspicions her attraction to him was the gift they have for seduction and she'd very much like to know if he was using it on her now.

Surprise took her as he opened the door to his place. The layout was the same as everyone else's. No special accommodations for the builder. It did reek of masculinity. Black leather couches, a bear skin rug and minimal decoration, but what was there, was defiantly manly. One lone painting was hung above a faux fireplace. It was of a Centaur.

"Who is that?" she asked, pointing at the portrait.

"My Great-Great Grandfather. He was a great warrior among our people. He was also a kind and gentle ruler. I've done everything in my power to live up to his legacy." Tucking his hands in his pockets, he nodded toward the kitchen. "Now, I'll go get that wine."

She watched as he walked over to his kitchen and gathered two stem-less wine glasses. He uncorked a bottle and filled the glasses before carrying them into the living room. "Please. Sit."

Finding a spot on the couch, she placed her purse on the table beside her. She ran her hands on the leather. "Faux leather?"

His husky chuckle made his large chest bounce. "God, no. We believe you honor the animal you just killed by adorning your home or yourself with clothing, weapons, shoes, décor and the like with anything you do not eat. This way the animal's sacrifice to feed us is honored by including nearly every part of the animal, instead of letting it rot. To toss away the skin and fur with the trash is just wrong."

"I agree." She felt a bit awkward asking such a question, but had little idea of how to strike up an easy conversation with the Centaur who had her so off balance.

He handed her a glass. "To new alliances."

"New alliances," she repeated before touching her glass to his. She took a sip and tried to hide her surprise as the sweet delicious flavor in the glass. This man could pick the wine! "Now, speaking of alliances, you do believe that honesty is the best policy among allies. Don't you?"

"Indeed." One eyebrow rose toward his blond curls.

"Then I will start with a bit of honesty. You make me uncomfortable."

His shoulders fell. "Really?"

She nodded. "That kiss, in the woods. I just meant to give you a quick peck and shut you up."

"But that's not what happened," he said as his lips

41

spread into a grin.

"No. It's not. And I find that troubling. Were you releasing whatever your special hormone is?" She eyed him.

He shook his head. "No. Not at all. I was in full control at the time."

After another sip of wine she placed her glass on the coffee table. "Your turn. Ask me a question."

His eyes widened. He took a giant gulp of wine before putting his glass next to hers. "I'm not sure what to ask."

It made her laugh. "Sure you are. There has to be something you want to know."

He turned toward her and put his arm on the back of the couch. "I see no bonding mark on you. Have you ever been mated?"

She shook her head, trying to hide how uncomfortable the question made her feel. But she'd asked for it. "I had a few short relationships, but there was never any real chemistry. My father tried to arrange a mating before he passed away, but that was during the last war and the Lycan passed in battle."

His lips curved downward as his look turned somber. "Did you mourn him?"

"I hadn't even met him yet." She leaned in, looking into his chocolate eyes. "Why do you keep flirting with me?"

His face reddened. "I've been drawn to you since the moment I laid eyes on you. The more I get to know about you, your personality, the more drawn I feel."

She'd never considered her own personality before.

As if reading her mind, he continued. "You're a natural caretaker, caring for your pack's every need. You mother others as if they were your own. I watched you closely. You never seem annoyed when anyone asks you for anything."

"That's your assessment?" The thought of him studying her made her heart leap. Stifling her grin wasn't working. She could feel her lips tightening as she fought it and assumed she must have looked amused.

"*So* far, yes." He rested the side of his head against his fist. "But I'd like to know more."

She picked up her glass, took another sip of wine to buy some time, and then turned to him. "That control you exercise. Are you doing it now?" She hoped he wasn't because if this was him controlling his hormones, she was in trouble. She could see his pecks through his tight black T-shirt and had thought about running her hands over them.

He nodded.

Damn.

"Okay, then stop." She needed to know, more than anything, if what she was feeling was natural or just a chemical reaction.

"What?" His mouth dropped.

Her heart rate sped up. "I don't want you on guard the whole time you're around me. Just stop whatever you're doing. I know somehow, it's making you uncomfortable. So...just relax and be yourself."

He straightened. "Um, no."

"No?" she gasped. "What do you mean, no?"

"It wouldn't be fair to you, Wendy. I don't want to do that to you."

She laughed at the absurdity of it. "How bad can it be? Z, just relax."

He stared at her, for what seemed like minutes. She hoped he'd just relax so she'd know what she was dealing with. Then...something changed. Her skin felt warm and damp with sweat. Her heart raced and her mouth watered. Her breasts felt heavy and swollen, like they'd jump out of her shirt. Heat pooled low in her belly causing desire to stir in her like she hadn't felt in ages.

"You see?"

Shifting in her seat, she took a fraction of a moment to gather herself. "Yeah, that's powerful stuff you have there.

But how do *you* feel?"

"Mate him, mark him. He is ours!" Her wolf pleaded.

His pearly white teeth flashed at her, adding to his allure. "Much better, thank you. How are *you*?"

"Actually, I'm a little more at ease now that I know you've been keeping that to yourself." She fanned her face. "You haven't tried to trick me, clearly." She giggled. Waves of excitement and euphoria were now washing over her. "Honestly, my wolf wants me to tear your clothes off and mark you as mine." *Dammit, I said that out loud.*

He scooted to the edge of the couch and stood. "I like the way your wolf thinks."

"Where are you going?"

He gave her a soft smile. "I keep hearing something. I'm going to the other room to check it out and give you some space to regain your composure. It's nice being able to let go of the hold I've had, but I don't want it influencing you too much. You'll just hate me for it later." Without waiting for her rebuttal, he left her in the living room.

Her wolf was panting away. She counted the weeks. *Not time for my heat.*

"Then it's safe to at least test him out." Her wolf urged. *"Just a little roll in the hay."*

Good grief, he's a living being, not something we test drive.

"Yeah, you want it too. I can feel you. You might erupt into flames soon." Her wolf tugged at her, prodding her.

"That's so weird," he said entering the room again. "I keep hearing voices, well a voice. But I can't tell where it's coming from."

She turned her ear in the direction he was facing as she tried to figure out to what he was referring. She hadn't heard a thing and great hearing was a benefit to being a Lycan. "What is it saying?"

He shook his head. "No. It's vulgar. I'm not repeating it. But I think someone is about to bond. Probably a Lycan."

She started to snicker at the thought of him hearing what her own inner wolf had to say. "Have you ever talked to your wolf side?"

"My what?"

She laughed again. "Don't you have a Centaur side? A being inside you that you can converse with?"

"I sure as hell hope not. The Centaur form is our natural form. We blend by being able to shift into human. The Lycan in me comes from my mother." He scratched his head. "You...have another voice inside your head?"

Trying to hide her amusement at what certainly had to be his wolf acting like hers, she smiled. "Seems like you do too, and he's a naughty little wolf."

He laughed and shook his head. "If only you knew."

She put her hand on his forearm. "Don't worry. My wolf is just as bad. Had me counting to see if I was going into heat." She snickered and rolled her eyes. "She actually suggested taking you for a spin...like we were test driving a car." Realizing how bad she must have sounded, she shook her head and held up her hands. "I'm sorry, she's really out of control right now. So if I burst into laughter for no reason, you'll know why."

She saw him tense, his shoulders rising. He sat a little stiffer.

"What's wrong?"

He shook his head. "I'm getting control of the situation."

"No, please. Just relax." She shook her head. "If I come to work here, we will be around each other a lot. I want you to relax around me. I'll figure out how to ignore it. Really." She tried to reassure him even if her sexual urges were driving her mad.

"So the wolf, I wonder why I've never heard him before?" He brushed a blonde curl out of his face.

"Probably because you don't spend much time in wolf form. Honestly, for a Lycan, our wolf is our closest confidant. They think differently than we do at times, which give you great introspection. They can be baser animals at times…sex, mating, procreation. Mine is going crazy because my sex life has been non-existent for many years." She silently cursed herself for blurting yet another intimate detail.

He rubbed his face. "Wendy, I'm fighting every urge I have right now. You can't say things like that."

Her smile quickly relaxed as she studied him seriously. "You know…it's not a bad idea."

"What?" He leaned back, his eyes wide.

"You know, trying each other out. Clearly there's some attraction here, but my natural instinct is to find a Lycan mate." She shrugged. "Maybe I've been looking in the wrong direction."

"Look at you, being so bold!" Her wolf mused. *"Good girl!"*

He sat silent; staring at her for a moment then smiled and shook his head. "Is this what they call informed consent?"

The thunder of her heart was nearly deafening in her ears. Her wolf was right. She'd never been this bold with anyone. "We're both adults."

He stood, holding out his hand. "It's time for me to take you back. Why don't you consider this when there is some distance between us?"

Doesn't he want me? "Oh, yes. It's getting late."

She grabbed up her purse, throwing it over her shoulder. She picked up the glass of wine and tossed it back. "Ready when you are."

The walk back to the others was a quiet one. She was afraid she'd either offended him, or come across as crass. Either way, she couldn't wait to get back to the comfort and safety of her cabin. She'd never been so bold, so forward before. Whether it was his powerful hormones or the duration of her unplanned celibacy, she didn't know, nor did she care. It was time for her to take control of her life. Zoltar and Colin had both made the same point. She always took care of everyone else. Maybe it was time for her to look out for her own needs.

FIVE

Wendy had made the affirmative decision to move to the school. Though her relationship with Zoltar had been left hanging in the wind, her future looked bright. She'd returned home from the tour and begun packing that night. Within a few days of her return, she was all packed up and ready to move to the school.

Easing her transition was the fact that Nala and Colin seemed to be getting along. Things were still quaint and not bonded, but they smiled more around each other and the tension had decreased. She'd even caught them holding hands a few times. The burden of leaving her brother behind was lessened by the chance that he might bond.

She had a nice, long cry the week prior. Sobbing every night, mourning the loss of the only pack she'd ever known. Grace had given her many counseling sessions.

"Wendy, we'll make a pack there. I promise. Roman and I are already your pack mates so you won't be completely alone. We'll run together each night until you feel comfortable. Okay?" Grace offered.

"How did you do it so quickly, Grace? I mean, here. How did you claim us so fast?"

She leaned against the truck and dusted her hands off on her jeans. Her auburn locks were pulling free from her pony tail. She tucked them behind her ears. "I admit my situation is a lot different. I'd never had a pack before, and this was my first real family to speak of. But...I made an honest effort to be part of it. I wanted it all. If you don't want this feeling of trepidation, then you have to try, every day, until you don't have to try anymore. That *one* day," She paused and closed her eyes briefly, smiled and continued, "that day when you think of the others as yours...then they are." She smiled. "It's part of our magic, I guess. The nice part for you is, you don't have to accept a new leader. You already think of Roman as your Alpha so things should be easy for you. Plus, Tiffany is transferring to our new school, so there's another familiar pack mate. "

She wiped her eyes one last time and took a deep breath. "Really, I couldn't do this without you, Grace. You've been a godsend."

Roman loaded the last box in the truck. "You ladies ready to start this new adventure?"

* * * *

An entire week had passed since she *offered herself* to Z. She hadn't had a chance to see him the next day or the following day after that before Grace and Roman dragged her back home, where she spent the time packing her things to make the final move. Because she owned so little things had moved fast for her. She'd been packed up and ready to move to the school to prepare for the coming opening long before Roman or Grace were ready. It'd given her time to observe her home and her brother with an open heart, a knowing it was time to let go. Nala and Colin seemed to be getting along, which made her choice to go an easier one. Things were still quaint and not bonded, but they smiled more around each other and the tension had decreased. She'd even caught them holding hands a few times. The burden of leaving her brother behind was lessened by the chance that he might bond.

Saying good-byes to Colin and Nada had been hard; it brought back the pain of her choice to leave, to start a life of her own. She had a nice, long cry. Sobbing most of drive back to the school, mourning the loss of the only pack she'd ever known.

She stepped out of the shower. It was desperately needed after loading and unloading all of her personal belongings. As she dried her hair, she kept playing over and over the words Grace had said to comfort her on their long drive back to school. *We'll make a pack there. I promise. Roman and I are already your pack mates so you won't be completely alone. We'll run together each night until you feel comfortable. Okay?*

She heaved a deep breath, "Okay Grace. I'm here. I'm making a real effort from this moment on."

As they'd loaded the truck, she'd asked Grace how she'd manage to make the change herself so quickly and claim the pack so fast. Grace smiled and leaned against the truck, dusting her hands off on her jeans; a habit that still made Wendy cringe, if she only knew how hard it was to get the black dirt out of those jeans.

She shook her head, realizing it would be hard to drop her *motherly*-type thinking, but the advice Grace had given was gold. Recalling the conversation brought her the comfort she sought. Grace had giving her that lazy grin as she'd said, *Wendy, I admit, my situation is a lot different. I'd never had a pack before, and this was my first real family to speak of. But...I made an honest effort to be part of it. I wanted it all. If you don't want this feeling of trepidation, then you have to try, every day, until you don't have to try anymore. That one day...that day when you think of the others as yours...then they are. It's part of our magic, I guess. The nice part for you is, you don't have to accept a new leader. You already think of Roman as your Alpha so things should be easy for you. Plus, Tiffany is transferring to our new school, so there's another familiar pack mate.*

Remembering those words brought tears to her eyes.

She wiped them away for the last time and took a deep breath then murmured as she looked in the mirror and combed out her wet hair, "I couldn't do this without you, Grace. You've been a godsend." She pulled on her robe and tied it closed as she headed for the bedroom. She sat on the new mattress the university has purchased for her and stared at the closet that housed all of her clothes. There was plenty of space to add more and with the salary she had been offered, it wouldn't be difficult to update her look.

She stood and picked up the sheets off the dresser and commenced in making up her new bed. It wasn't difficult to notice someone had made themselves scarce while she moved in. That same someone had made themselves scarce since the last time she'd been at the school—and had offered an interesting proposition. As she pulled the comforter toward the headboard, she jumped—startled by a knock at her door.

"Coming!" she called out as she hurried toward the door. When she opened it, Zoltar stood there with a bottle of wine. Her eyes traveled the lot of him, from his blonde locks, down his tight T-shirt that was stretched to accommodate beautiful pectorals, down his jeans, clear to his loafers.

"Thought you could use a nightcap after a long, taxing day." His smile was wide, his teeth brilliant white set off by the tan that had darkened from working outdoors.

"Oh, I'm a mess. I wish I would have known you were coming," she fussed with her hair. Of course he would show up looking sexy as hell when she was a total mess. That was her best luck.

"Nonsense," he said as he walked in, "but if it would make you feel better, I'll open this while you go put something more comfortable on."

Closing the door, she uttered her dismay as she ran off toward the bedroom. She looked at her closet...a nightgown seemed inappropriate, but dressing in jeans seemed silly this time of night. She snatched a pair of yoga pants off the shelf and yanked them on, following up with a thin hoody. She looked at herself in the mirror. "Casual but not too frumpy, I guess."

She wound her hair in a loose bun and crammed a pencil through it that was sitting on her dresser before taking a deep breath and making her way to the living area.

He handed her a glass of blush wine as she took a seat. "Better?"

"Yes, thank you."

"I tried to give you some peace while you moved in. However, I couldn't let you think I was ignoring you. But first, a toast." He held up his glass. She did the same. "To new beginnings and adventures."

She touched her glass to his before taking a sip.

"Wendy," he said then cleared his throat, "before I release the hold I have on myself, let me first say I didn't come here to get lucky."

She knew he wasn't joking, but it seemed like the perfect ice breaker. It made her laugh. "But you want to know if I made up my mind?"

"In a matter of speaking, yes."

"It was my proposition and no, I haven't changed my mind. I'm not exactly into casual sex, but I still feel the same as I did before." As soon as the last word crossed her lips, she felt everything change. Her body instantly reacted to the hormone he released. She gasped quietly and cursed herself for telling him she wanted him to relax around her.

"Thank you. Now, did you get settled okay?" he leaned back on the couch.

She felt as if she'd burst open like an overwatered tomato. Her heart, her breathing, her mind...everything raced. "Yes. I didn't have much to move. Everything in here is new but my clothes and even then, I'm going to have to get some attire for teaching before the session begins. Grace said something about classes for us?"

His smile caused his eyes to crease at the sides. "Yes,

we'll get a bit of a taste of what the kids will be going through for about a month." He leaned back a bit more, crossing his ankle over his knee. "Plus we need to learn some teaching skills. Three of the professors we hired are experienced human college professors. They're going to show us how to make our own syllabuses according to state guidelines and how to run our classes. I think it'll be quite fun."

She feigned a cough to disguise her panting breath. Heat radiated through the hoody and she swore steam must be coming out around her neck. "Well, Xander gave me a crash course on using the new laptop. That kid is good. I think Grace said something about him getting a degree and teaching computer technologies here. He has me feeling like a pro in a short time. Don't get me wrong, I surfed the internet plenty before, but that's all."

He poured a bit more wine in his glass. "More?"

"Not yet." She'd only taken a sip. There was no room in the glass for more, but she appreciated the gesture. Her body was still reacting to him, but she did notice the static energy feeling was easing, just slightly.

"Can we talk about the real issue with us?" she blurted.

His eyes widened. He took a big drink of wine.

So did she.

"That's probably a good idea."

She leaned forward, resting her elbows on her knees. After another sip of wine, she let the glass rest on the table. "Our kinds haven't really been allies. My kind, Lycans…we haven't really taken to blending with other species. Our beautician has a Fae boyfriend and that was a huge step. Colin wasn't the most popular guy when he approved it. That was back when he was the Alpha of our pack." She waved her hands. "Anyway, I'm not sure if we became…a couple that it would be that well received. Everyone seems to want all of our kinds to unite, but that's just on the surface. Mating with a Centaur could make me an outcast and Lycans are pack people. I can't say the same about Centaurs...I just don't know that much about your kind."

His head bobbed as he clung to her every word.

"You took my breath away the first moment I saw you, but I figured it was because of what you are. Then you showed an interest in me and quite frankly, I'm not sure what your motives are, other than sexual draw."

He opened his mouth.

She continued before he could speak. "Beyond sex. We all have a sexual motive. Every single stinkin' one of us. So I'm not being judgmental." She paused. "But to be absolutely, undeniably clear, I have zero desire to be a Centaur incubator."

He laughed so loud it startled her. He reached over and patted her knee. "I'm sorry. That was...that hurt, but it was funny at the same time. I don't want you to incubate anything." He put his hand over his mouth for a moment and regained his composure. "I have many of the same concerns. I want you to have a home and a pack. I don't want to put you in any position you don't want to be in. I cannot put into words the pull I have felt toward you. It has been a misnomer that all Centaurs want is sex. We are sexual beings, don't get me wrong. But we have all craved a mate. As you probably guessed, I've had ample opportunity for sex. I have, however, remained celibate because the only desire I have, is for you. That's a new experience for me." He picked up his wine, chugged it down and refilled his glass. "However, I would like to date you, Wendy. I don't want to have sex with you sometimes and call it good. I think about you every moment, of every day. I think about your vanilla aroma, how it invades my senses every time we're near. I think about your haunting blue eyes, how they bore right through me. I think about your kindness, and need to care for others. Your laugh is what dances in my thoughts as I sleep. Mostly...mostly, I think about our one and only kiss...how sweet you tasted on my lips."

"And when you are in heat, the Pixies have protection that feels like nothing. If that's not suitable, then we may use whatever you wish, because the only child I have...I want to be with my mate."

Time for talk had passed. She leaned in toward him, and placed her hand on his neck. She pulled him in closer, brushing her lips lightly across his.

"*A mate! Yes! A mate! Finally!*" Her wolf danced around with joy.

With the softness of a butterfly, he grazed her bottom lip with his tongue and he scooped his arm around her back pulling her onto him.

Wearing yoga pants, she could feel every inch of him growing...thickening...hardening beneath her. She worried, briefly, about being out of practice. Instinct however, was all that was needed. She pulled her fingers through the back of his locks as their lips caressed. She pulled him closer to her, though there was no more room to give. Her breasts were planted firmly on his chest as his kiss trailed from her mouth down the nape of her neck.

He stood, taking her with him and then carried her to the bedroom. Placing her on the bed, he stared down at her for a moment before unbuttoning his pants, letting them fall to the floor.

Commando! Nice. She reveled in his nude form, thinking he could pose as Atlas, holding the Earth on his shoulders.

Climbing onto the bed next to her, rolling to his side, he quickly reclaimed their kiss.

She didn't remember him unzipping her hoody but found her breasts free from her shirt and now claimed by his strong hands. She pulled at his shoulder and he followed her lead, rolling to top of her. Pulling his black T-shirt over his head, he tossed it aside. He kissed his way between her breasts, not stopping to pleasure them, but moving around them, leaving the nipple taught and wanting.

He kissed his way down her stomach, nibbling along

her left hip bone, then her right. She wanted more. She wanted him to manhandle her most needy areas and he was leaving her wanting. She turned her hips up, exposing her yoga pant covered mound, begging with need. He kissed her inner thigh through the thin stretchy material, using his lips to lightly pinch the delicate skin. It drove her wild. His hands cupped her breasts from the sides, still leaving her nipples untouched.

Oh my God, please.

With tantalizing alacrity, he placed his mouth around her now swollen and needy clit and rolled it between his lips. She whined at the slightest pleasure he gave her. "Hmm, more."

Releasing her breasts, he began dragging his fingers down her sides before he tucked his them in her waistband, pulling her pants just below her bottom. He touched her clit once and then twice with his warm, wet tongue.

Her skin was ablaze with need and adrenaline. She didn't even care about foreplay anymore. She just wanted his thick, hard cock buried deep within her. It was too much, the torture. She wanted to scream. It has been so long since she'd been with a man. Her body ached for him to be inside her. She was dampening more with each tiny little torture.

When he blew cool air on her clit and she felt one quick and tiny spasm. Her body was begging for more than she was getting.

"Please," she gasped.

He chuckled. "Your first time with me is going to be like nothing you've experience. I don't want you to ever forget it." He sat up and yanked her yoga pants off, tearing them in half at the crotch. "Don't worry. I will replace them." He grinned down at her before looping one end around her ankle. Before she could figure out what he was up to, he hand her ankles fastened together. It was tight, but painless.

"What the—"

"You can tell me to stop at any time." He bound her wrists then tied the torn yoga pants to the head board.

He made his way on top of her and scooped his arm between her lower back and the bed. He twisted and she was on top of him, her clit resting on his cock.

"Show me how much you want it."

Her ankles were bound tight, barely letting her knees open enough to let him between them. She wiggled, causing friction against her hood. She continued wiggling up and down, his hardness giving her clit some much needed attention.

As she moved, her sensitive nipples grazed his chest hair. The yoga pants stretched only enough to give her an inch or two to move. "Damn," she complained. It felt tremendous, but it wasn't enough.

Why wasn't this man inside her yet?

"That's it, Wendy. Fuck me with your clit." His voice was low, primal and sexy.

She pulled hard on the headboard, the fabric stretching, lifting her enough; she placed her needy nipple on his lip, then slid down so her swollen nub could get some relief.

"God, it's like having an itch I can't scratch!" She complained. She continued rubbing her clit against him and teasing his lips with her nipple until she cried out. "Please, just take me!"

Reaching down, he moved the head of his cock to her opening. "I'm all yours," he whispered.

She felt him at her opening, starting to penetrate her outer walls. Inching herself down on him through the challenge of legs that were barely open and being bound, she gasped as his swollen cock entered her.

He released the bindings freeing her wrists from the headboard but still bound. He ducked his head inside, allowing her elbows to rest by his ears. "Are you ready?"

"Z please!"

He popped his legs out from under her so they were on

the outside of her thighs and pumped into her from below. He took her left nipple into his mouth and sucked slightly, rolling the bud with his tongue.

"More!"

He pushed faster, grabbing her ass as leverage. With her legs closed tight, everything felt amplified as his long hard cock made its way in and out of her. Crying out, she fought to hold onto something, anything, as he drove into her.

An explosion of color blinded her eyes as her walls clenched around him. She struggled to catch her breath as he slowed his thrusts from below while she rode the wave downward. Just as she started to recover from her orgasm, he rolled her to the side. He pulled her up so she was resting on her hands and knees before entering her again.

Her insides still electrified from her orgasm, ignited once again as he thrust into her from behind. A moment later he pushed into her and stayed, spilling his seed as he gasped. After a few moments rest he withdrew and fumbled with the shredded pants, untying them to use them to clean her.

It was unexpected.

It was gentle.

It was sweet.

They both collapsed on the bed.

SIX

When she opened her eyes, the sun was pouring through her window, illuminating Zoltar's hair and skin. She felt a smile widen her lips. *It wasn't a dream.* She inched away from him and crept into the closet, slipping into a pair of track pants and a tank before tiptoeing to the kitchen. She smiled as she filled the brew basket of the coffee maker. If this move meant she could transition from a lonely bachelorette to frequent sex like she'd had last night, she decided she'd adjust just fine.

"Wendy!" Grace was screaming in her head. *"Are you okay?"*

"Grace?" she said aloud.

"Oh my God. Meeting in the dining hall in five."

She shuddered, knowing Grace had special powers with her royal blood but having her inside her head was unsettling. She had anticipated waking her lover with a fresh cup of coffee and conversation. This wasn't what she'd had in mind.

Rushing into the bedroom, she shook her slumbering Centaur awake.

"Huh?" He sat up rubbing his eyes.

"There's some sort of meeting in the dining hall in five minutes. It must be an emergency. Grace sounded kind of frantic. We'd better get cleaned up. There's coffee in the kitchen." She jumped in the shower while he headed to the kitchen for a quick cup. The moment she stepped out he was in and out in seconds.

He dried off and pulled his jeans up as fast as he could. "Emergency? Did she say what kind?"

"No."

He snatched his shirt off the floor and ran out of her place, slamming the door behind him.

"Good morning to you too." She sighed as she grabbed a pair of tennis shoes and socks and carried them to the kitchen, sliding them on before grabbing a cup of coffee to take with her. She hurried toward the dining area, taking quick sips of the brew while it was hot.

She rounded the corner into the dining hall and saw a group of Pixies sobbing. *Oh shit. This is bad.*

"Wendy! I'm so glad you're okay," Grace ran to her and flung her arms around her shoulders. She managed not to spill a drop of coffee.

"What's going on?"

"One of the Pixies was murdered last night. There was a note. Apparently, there are some factions that aren't very happy about us all living under the same roof. They want us to stay separated."

It was then she saw what the group of sobbing men and women were standing around. On the floor, lying on a board was a nearly decapitated female with a note nailed to her chest.

"Is everyone else accounted for?" Zoltar's voice boomed throughout the hall.

Roman walked over to him. His face was drawn and he looked pale. "We're waiting on a few Dwarves to arrive. But other than that, yes."

A Centaur in his natural form galloped into the hall with a dozen gnomes on his back. "All of the gnomes are accounted for, Sir."

Zoltar lifted them off of his brother's back and placed them on the floor, two at a time. Wendy appreciated how gently he handled them.

Roman shook his head. "We're really going to have to ramp up security. We can't have this happening to our students." He took a deep breath. "I will speak with Gustav. Vampires can cover the night shifts."

"My men will rotate the daylight hours along with the Dwarves. They're voracious warriors." Zoltar looked to his brother. They both nodded. She wondered if that was his Beta.

"Damn straight we're warriors. No one is getting hurt on our watch!" The last two of them cursed as they walked into the hall.

"What can I do?" she asked, feeling helpless.

Grace rubbed her face. "We are all going to start running together to strengthen the pack bond. Don't run without at least one other person with you. Okay? I just couldn't stand it if something happened to you." Tears spilled down her cheeks. "She was a gentle soul."

"Get her body laid to rest immediately. We can't have a corpse lying here when the humans arrive." Roman said in a low voice to Zoltar. He turned, raised his voice to address everyone else. "We shall pay our respects after dinner. For now, let's return her to Mother Earth where she can rest peacefully."

Four Pixie men lifted the board the body was on. They hung their heads as they carried her out of the room.

Her gaze immediately fell to the pool of blood on the floor where the Pixie's body had rested. When she looked up, she noticed several others staring as well. While things had been tense, for most supernaturals, there hadn't been a bloody battle in decades. Blood took getting used to, especially that of a pack mate. The last war had given Wendy an iron stomach. Gore just didn't shock her anymore.

"Grace, where are the cleaning supplies?" she asked before she downed the rest of her coffee. She needed to get the blood off of the floor and assumed that everyone else needed it gone as soon as possible as well.

"In the kitchen is a storage closet. Thank you, Wendy." She sobbed and fell back on a bench.

"You're taking this awfully hard. How well did you know her?"

Wiping her tears on the backs of her hands, she cleared the lump in her throat. "When I became...this, I felt a natural protection for all of nature's creatures. I would weep as much for a vampire I'd only just met. I have no control. I feel like...like I lost a child."

Her heart sank. She could not wrap her head around caring so much for total strangers. But it was clear, it had touched Grace deeply.

"I'll get this cleaned up." She put her cup on the table and hurried into the kitchen. After a bit of searching, she found the closet and gathered a bucket, scrub brush, rags and cleaner. She filled the bucket with water and carried everything to the stain on the floor. She wasted no time, attempting to get as much of the blood up as she could before it dried.

"You shouldn't be doing that," Zoltar said as he knelt down.

"No one should." She shook her head. "Poor soul."

The warmth of his hand seeped into her arm. "I'm sorry for running out so quickly."

She held up her hand. "Stop. This was an emergency. It's fine. We'll talk later. I'm sure you have something important to do."

He nodded. "You're okay?"

Looking up at him, she shook her head and in a low voice said, "I'd like to sink my teeth into whatever beast attacked that poor girl, but other than that, I'm fine."

"Agreed."

Once there was no trace of blood left, she dumped and

cleaned the bucket then put everything away. She noticed someone was missing…Grace's friend from college. She spotted Grace walking out of the hall and ran to her.

"Grace? Have you checked on your friend, Barb?"

She turned around. "I'm sorry. What?"

"Your friend, is she okay? I didn't see her here."

Looking away, Grace gazed at the floor. "Barb's mother was murdered. She didn't want to be exposed to the body. She stayed in her room."

After closing her eyes and taking a deep breath, she scooped Grace's hand in hers. "Come on. You don't need to be in here. Go see your friend. I'm sure she's shaken up and you could probably use a bit of comfort, yourself."

Grace hugged her tight before releasing her and headed down the hall.

Her natural instinct had been to care for and nurture her pack. She'd cook, clean, organize and counsel. But now, in this new position, she had no idea what her duties were. She did the only responsible thing she could do. She went back to her living quarters and grabbed up a manuscript on Lycanthropy. She clicked her pen, ready to take notes on her legal pad. Her class would not get a second rate education from her.

Before she could get past the first page, there was a knock on her door. She rushed to answer it.

"Hi Wendy!" Xander stepped in. "I have your new laptop and your smartphone. I have synchronized the calendar on your phone and your laptop because I know how much you love organization. I also know how excited you are to use technology," he teased.

"Xander!" She threw her arms around him.

"Uh…hi." He stood stiff as she hugged him.

After she released him she gave him a once over. Every brown curl was in place. "You need to eat more. Are you okay after what happened here?"

With a nod and a shrug, he let out a sigh. "I didn't know her. I guess I am a bit creeped out though. Anyway, let me show you the note taking feature. It'll organize your notes into subjects so you can find what you type in when you need to."

He pulled the laptop out of his bag and placed it on the table. He clicked around showing her where to find what she needed.

"Seems easy enough."

"It's good to see you, Wendy. Do you need anything before I go?"

She looked at the young Lycan man. He hadn't integrated to the pack so easily, but was eager to right that wrong since the return of his mother. Still, he seemed awkward most of the time. "No, no, you go take care of business. I have some reading to get done."

"Oh, you have a message on your phone." He showed her a group text message. "Grace has decided to have lunch on the lawn since..." He paused. At a loss for words he shrugged.

"That's a great idea. Thank you." She smiled as she opened the door for him.

"Thank you for always being so nice to me. I know I was a bit of a pain in the ass before but you always took care of me, even when I was in a mood." His lips tightened into a thin line.

With a smile she patted him on the shoulder. "It's my pleasure."

As soon as he was gone she sat down with the laptop and her book. "Okay, Mr. Computer Thing. You and me, we're going to get along. No fussing." She resumed her place reading and making notes.

* * * *

Most of the residents were quiet at lunch, though the Pixies were notably absent. There was some talk of a mourning ritual keeping them away. Zoltar had taken a seat on the blanket with Wendy, Grace and Roman. They kept the conversation light until everyone was finished with the meal.

"As much as I want to respect the loss of life here, we really do need to get back on schedule." Grace rubbed her forehead. "The humans are a little freaked out too and it took a lot for me to convince them we aren't a bunch of barbarians."

Zoltar's jaw clenched as he stared at the blanket. "We should start our normal schedule tomorrow. Let the new professors begin their classes. Order must be maintained."

"I think it's important that we start the pack runs. We need to start bonding." Wendy sat a little straighter. "The hardest part for me was leaving the pack, worrying about integrating here, fear of loneliness…I'm willing to bet I am not the only one who had that fear. As you pointed out to me, Grace, we need to start looking at everyone as our pack."

A gentle smile spread across Roman's face. "That is why you're an asset. We'll all go for a run as soon as the sun sets. The four of us will go and invite the others."

"We need to invite Ella. She just lost one of her people. I don't want her retreating to only her kind for comfort. Let's show her we're her family too…that we support her." Grace knotted her fingers. "God, but Pixies don't run—not like we do.

Standing from the blanket, Wendy grabbed her things. "Let her mourn today. Tomorrow, you two use your special memories or whatever to figure out how to bond with them as a pack." She fanned her finger at Roman and Grace.

Zoltar looked at them, then at Wendy. "Special memories?"

As he stood, Roman helped Grace to her feet. "When we mated, we received the blood memories of our ancestors. It was a lot of information and it doesn't all come to the front of our minds immediately. But I just had a recollection. They don't bond the way other packs do.

They're more human. They need time, meals together, and a feeling of comradery."

"Oh, I was raised human. I can help with that." Grace grabbed Roman's hand. "I need to get to work. See you for dinner?"

Zoltar scooped up the blanket and folded it. "What are you going back to?"

She studied his bronze skin, glistening in the sunlight, stretched over muscular arms. His golden blond curls falling over his forehead called out for her fingers to dance through them. She shook her head. "Reading. I was reading."

He grinned. "Good thing I'm in control right now, eh?"

Laughing she shook her head. "Indeed. And you? What are you doing?"

"Absolutely nothing. My plans for today were shot down the drain with the morning events. What are you reading?"

She looped her arm in his and walked toward the building. "The vampires gave me the first book written on Lycans. It's a detailed account of our history, our physiology and psychology. It's quite riveting, actually." With a gentle squeeze to his arm, she continued. "I've studied our kind most of my life. This book was written by a Lycan and a Vampire prior to the first war. We started off as allies. I really don't know when or how we became enemies, but I'm glad that is over. It really is amazing to see everyone working and living together."

Beauregard's seven foot frame came to an abrupt halt in front of them, blocking their entrance into the castle. "Z, I'm going to be questioning some of the residence about the Pixie. I was wondering if I could borrow one of your men. I think a Fae and a Centaur will be enough to scare the truth out of someone."

He bowed his head slightly, "I think you'll find Prometheus quite persuasive and we are willing to do whatever we need to do to get down to the bottom of this." His shoulders pulled back. "We thank you for including one of the herd."

The Fae King's laugh was loud and booming...yet eerie. "Don't thank me yet. *Everyone* is a suspect."

"As it should be," Wendy interrupted. "Everyone should be questioned about their whereabouts. Nothing like that should ever happen." She fought the urge to blink as her head swam. A bit of anger bubbled in her chest, confusing her further.

His crystal blue eyes danced as he smiled down at her. "I agree, Ms. Baker. Pardon my intrusion; try to enjoy the remainder of the day."

As the Fae walked away from them, she gave a shudder.

Zoltar stood back and eyed her. "You okay?"

"I felt a bit dizzy for a moment...then a little angry." She waved her hands in front of her face. "I'm being silly. Ignore me."

"You're not being silly." He patted her arm. "He was searching your mind to see if you had any ill feelings toward the others. He dug swift but deep. It'll leave you feeling off balance. He's the most powerful Fae I've ever met, which is probably why he is the king."

She had nothing to hide and had no fears of the Fae King discovering that for himself. "Let's go in."

When they entered the building, his gaze fell on a group of gnomes who looked exhausted. "Need a lift?" he asked.

A little female wiped the back of her hand on her forehead. "Thanks, Z. It takes us forever to get anywhere in this castle."

"Motorized cars!" The words flew out of Wendy's mouth before she had time to consider them.

"What?" Zoltar asked with a snicker.

"Come on, Engineer. You know, those little toy cars. Can't we retrofit them for the Gnomes?" She smiled as she lifted two of them in one arm. "You guys know what I'm talking about?"

"I'm Mary," one of them said to her. "And I would love a car. It took us an hour just to get to lunch. We can't waste that kind of time now that we're on a schedule in this huge castle."

"Well, Mary," Zoltar nodded and smiled, "I think our Headmistress is onto something. It wouldn't be hard to retrofit the stairs with ramps. I'll have to stabilize the steering. Those little cars are all over the place. But with that and more battery life…we might have a viable means of transportation for you."

The gnomes gave them directions to their rooms. The two didn't hesitate to run into town after a short stop to report to Grace where they were going.

"This really is brilliant," he said as they strolled through the toy aisle.

She filled the carts with every motorized toy car that he suggested would be viable. "There's what—thirty of them or so? This should be enough. We have five backups."

"There's a hardware store next door. I can get the rest of what I need there." He paid the bill and they filled the moving truck with their purchases before heading over to the hardware store. She watched as he carefully selected tiny gears, springs, wire and rechargeable battery packs. He continually did calculations on a small notepad before selecting each piece. When she snuck a peek at his tablet, it looked like hieroglyphics. She had no idea what any of it meant.

Finally at the checkout counter, the lady behind the register stared at him like he was a god. "Find everything you need?"

"Yeah," he said looking at the pile on the counter.

"Everything?" she asked leaning in, squeezing her boobs together.

Wendy could not contain her laugh.

The gaze of the cashier shifted to Wendy, narrowed

and full of anger.

"Z, are you sure you found...*everything*?" she mocked.

He smiled at her and rolled his eyes.

Looking back to the items on the counter, the teller fanned herself as she scanned the items.

When the bill was paid and they were outside, she let it go. She leaned over and put her hands on her knees as she belly laughed.

"What is so funny?"

"That human!" She stood up and wiped her eyes. "If she had any clue...if you would have let your hormones go, she would have ripped her shirt off right there."

He shook his head and placed his hand on her back, giving her a gentle push forward. "I'm glad you find this amusing."

"*Everything*...like perhaps boobs were on sale, and her shit was half off!" She laughed as she climbed in the truck.

Relenting with a laugh of his own, he shook his head. "Okay, okay, I can see how funny it is to you. You don't live with it. It's really annoying after decades."

After the truck roared to life, he put it in gear, and grabbed her hand. "Since you're not too busy, would you mind helping me with this project?"

Her phone chimed. She dug in her bag and pulled it out. "Looks like it'll be an after-dinner project. My phone tells me we are about to be late." She shook her head. "Xander really thinks I need an alarm for everything."

When they arrived at the castle, he had two of his men help carry the load into his office. Each of them eyed Wendy, making her stomach tense. Did they not appreciate the fact that she had captured the eye of their king? Wasn't she good enough?

Dinner was in the dining hall, which had been set with several candelabras to set the mood. They found empty seats and filled their plates.

"What were you two up to?" Theron asked as he shoveled a spoon full of pudding in his mouth.

And now his Beta is asking questions. They really don't like me.

"Shopping," Zoltar answered as he sawed into his ham steak.

Theron dropped his spoon. "Z, I was being serious."

He smiled. "So was I."

Theron leaned back in his chair and looked at her. "You had him shopping? What have you done to our King?"

She winked, hoping to gain his friendship. "Don't worry. We went to the hardware store."

"They bought a bunch of toys and electrical shit," one of Z's men said. "We just took it all to his office."

"Toys?" Theron scratched his head.

She looked at Zoltar for some cue. Why was he being evasive? "Why don't you just answer him already?"

Roman approached and took a seat. "Z, what is this about transportation?"

Theron looked at everyone around him as if he hoped to piece together a complicated puzzle.

"The Gnomes," she started in an effort to quell the uneasy feeling she was having, "are having a difficult time navigating this large property in a timely fashion. So, I had an idea and Z is running with it. We bought a bunch of toy jeeps that should work."

Zoltar reached in his pocket and pulled out his notepad. He ripped out two of the small sheets and handed them to Theron. "I want every stairwell fitted with these ramps and small guard rails."

"Wendy!" Roman slapped the table. "That's damned brilliant."

She shook her head, happy to have another ally at the table. "They shouldn't have to be carried around like children. It's going to get demeaning and look," she pointed to the dining entry where a group of exhausted Gnomes shuffled in, "they're just now making it to dinner and they look absolutely exhausted. It takes their tiny legs so long to carry them. It just seems humane."

As they walked up the ramp to their table, every single one looked like they'd pass out from exhaustion. They dragged their feet. Their heads hung and their shoulders slumped forward. She scooted back from her chair, walked over to their table and knelt on the floor near them. "I know you're all so tired. But can I have one volunteer to work with Z and me on your cars?"

Mary stood up. "I'll do it!"

She smiled at the little woman. "Thank you very much. I'll come back in a bit when you've had a chance to eat."

"It doesn't take long to fill my belly." She waved her hand in the air. "I'll be ready in five minutes."

A thought had occurred to her, one of pack mentality. "Have you ever run with a Lycan?"

Dropping to her knees, the tiny woman looked up at her, exasperated. "Are you messing with me? Look at my legs."

She winked. "Five minutes. I'll be back." And she was. She carried the little Gnome on her shoulder as she walked with Grace, Roman, and Zoltar to the tree line. "After I shift, climb on by my neck and hold on to my fur as tight as you need to. Don't worry, you can't hurt me." She placed the little creature on the ground and shifted. Once in wolf form she nodded and squatted for the little one to climb on her.

Mary hugged on to her neck. "Don't drop me."

As soon as the others shifted they started off along a path that had already been cut. She remained conscience of the tiny fragile being that screamed and giggled while holding on for dear life.

"It was so good of you to bring her. Look how much fun she's having." Grace's voice came through loud and clear.

When the run was over, she bowed so her passenger could safely climb down, then she shifted.

"Did you like it? It wasn't too hard to hold on, was it?" she asked as she picked Mary up and placed her on her shoulder.

"That must be how humans feel on roller coasters. It was scary and fun all at the same time." She leaned her head against Wendy's. "Thank you."

"Ready to work on these cars?" Zoltar smiled at Mary.

"Oh yes! I'm more awake than I have been in a week!"

* * * *

They'd worked for two hours on the first car, having Mary test out each feature as they went along. Without adjustable seats, they had to make the steering column longer and put an actual footboard in the little vehicle. Zoltar had managed to rig up the throttle on the dash at first, then with a spring and some wire put it on the floor like a normal car.

She zipped around his office and soon drove like she'd been doing it her whole life. However long that was.

"We'll take you down to the main floor. Then you can drive your car back to your living quarters. I'll finish the rest of them up tomorrow for everyone else now that I know what I need to do." He stretched his neck. "The ramps should be done by the end of day tomorrow. Theron is very good about delegating work for maximum efficiency. So your people won't be so exhausted every day."

"What about the battery things?" Mary asked.

"We'll deliver them. Everyone should keep a spare here," he said pointing to the trunk. "So when the first battery dies, you have a fresh one to swap out."

Wendy stood and stretched. It was then she noticed the drawings on the wall—blueprints for the school, all hand drawn. Each measurement has been penciled in. "Z? You planned out this entire project by hand?"

He nodded at her as he picked up the little car. "Yeah. I didn't sleep for a week."

It was then that she realized how taken he had been with the project. He'd mentioned how proud they should be about the integration…the school. This project held meaning for him that she'd not recognized before. He built a school that reflected the beauty of an idea…an idea that they could all live with one another in peace and a future for his people.

She walked along the wall, gazing at each page. He had fortified the structure to withstand weather, time and serious use. He had a wind map attached to one, storm history to another. There were pages of statistics on thermal values of stone versus wood.

"That's why the living spaces are more enclosed. There won't be outside drafts making us cold." He pointed to an aerial map. "The wind turbines are over here, so they're not an eyesore on the property."

"Guys?" Mary interrupted. "I'm really exhausted."

Wendy scooped her up. "Let's get you to the main floor."

She carried Mary as one would a child at first, on her hip. "Oh dear, I'm sorry. This must be awkward for you." She moved to switch Mary to her shoulder.

"No. It's nice. You're warm and I'm so tired." Mary kissed her cheek. "You're very sweet, Lycan. I always thought you guys were so scary—that you would eat us."

The absurdity made her laugh. "Well then you relax. I'll carry you downstairs and you can get to bed. You're my friend now. We're all friends. Lycans don't really want to go around eating Gnomes."

"Where were you last night? No one can account for your whereabouts." A Centaur that must have been Prometheus had cornered a Dwarf in the hall. Beauregard stared at him, potentially digging into his brain the way he had done to Wendy.

She elbowed Zoltar and nodded in their direction.

Zoltar chuckled as he carried the car. "Almost there."

Interrogation is not that entertaining!

When they reached the main floor, Mary climbed in her little car and drove off toward her apartment. They watched with smiles on their faces.

"We did a good thing today," he said as he put her arm around her shoulder.

"We did. Considering how the day started, I'm quite happy with how it ended. Why did you laugh at those two interrogating that Dwarf?"

His big shoulders rose and fell. "A Centaur and a Fae interrogating a Dwarf? That's overkill. But Dwarves have never had anything against Pixies. It wasn't a Dwarf that killed her or the angle of the cut would have been much different."

"That doesn't explain the chuckle." She chewed her lip, hoping she hadn't started a relationship with a sociopath.

"We are working together. Never in the history of the world has a Fae King and a Centaur stood shoulder to shoulder for any reason. It's just...I don't know, it seems so odd. Like a cat and dog as best friends. It happens, but it's still a bit ironic. Right?"

"Yeah, I have to tell you, if those two interrogated me, I'd probably tuck tail and run." She smiled. "Okay, I can see the humor, especially since Dwarves aren't known for backing down."

They headed toward their own living spaces.

"I want to build them actual cars. Those little toys weren't meant for constant transportation. They're pretty flimsy." He rubbed his neck. "But that will have to wait."

When they reached her door, she half expected him to follow her inside. To her disappointment, he gave her a short, sweet kiss goodnight and left.

SEVEN

Wendy sat through a class led by Ms. Rutger. She instructed on creating a syllabus, grading, and exams. Diligent as always, she took notes, and paid close attention.

"Those of you teaching core subjects must stick to the guidelines for what freshman, sophomores, juniors, and seniors all need to pass by the end of year exams. This is important for us to maintain our status as an accredited university, albeit a private one. A four year degree program is serious and employers out there take it very seriously. Our job is to educate and prepare them for the big bad world."

The Lycans in the room laughed.

"Why is that funny?" she asked.

Wendy stood, trying to hide her smile. "You just made a big bad wolf reference, sort of."

Ms. Rutger nodded as if dismissing her. "Moving along, those of you teaching non-standard or elective classes have a bit more leeway, but in the packet I've handed you, you'll see that you have guidelines to follow as well. Take some time this evening to get acquainted." She continued with

75

her instructions.

Three hours later, her mind was numb and she was filing out of class next to Zoltar. "Lunch couldn't come soon enough. I can't handle one more piece of information."

He shrugged with half a smile. "It was a lot."

Mary and two other Gnomes zipped by them in their new cars. He looked at her with a tender smile that made her feel warm inside. "Someone is having fun."

"And they'll beat us to lunch for the first time."

She heard the ping of hammers hitting chisels and followed the sound, pleased to see the Dwarves carving hall numbers in stone. "It's getting close."

"Yes it is. Finishing touches today and tomorrow then construction will finally reach completion." He grabbed her hand. "It's about to begin...the adventure."

She looked up at his bronze face which beamed with what looked like pride, maybe a little excitement. It was infectious.

The lunch hall was buzzing with activity when they arrived. The Pixies were back, though they didn't have the same spring in their step as usual. She watched as they slowly ate, staring at their plates. She knew she couldn't erase their loss, but there had to be something she could do.

Roman had mentioned comradery. The Pixies needed to feel as if they were a part of something. She finished her soup and swallowed the rest of her sandwich. She pulled her phone out of her bag and walked over to Xander who studied the dessert table.

"Hey Xander, I was wondering if you could help me?" She held her phone out to him. "I remember you saying something about this playing music."

He smiled and took a step closer so he was next to her. "Press that button then search by genre."

"Thank you." She walked to the front of the hall and searched until she found some happy Irish music. Once the music started, she held out her hand to a Pixie male who stared in return. His ocean blue eyes widened as he flipped his jet black hair out of his face.

Please. Please let this work.

He slid his hand into hers and stood, stomping his feet. He let go and flung the crook of his elbow into hers and started dancing. She hadn't danced this particular dance in a quarter of a century, and while she fumbled, she did notice others getting up to join. By the end of the song, all of the Pixies, the Gnomes, and most of the Centaurs and Lycans danced. There was a lot of laughter and a round of applause.

Grace beamed at her, clapping. *"Yes, my friend, you belong here."*

Her heart swelled with pride. With the approval of her Queen, she gave Grace an affirmative nod and grabbed her things to head off to her room. Class had been exhausting and she was relieved they were giving them a long lunch to recuperate.

Once in her room, she dropped her books on the coffee table and fell on the couch. She stared at the pile of material, feeling more overwhelmed than she could ever recall. To top it off, part of her duties were to arrange the schedules of every incoming student.

"Guess I'll sleep on Tuesdays." She leaned back on the couch and looked at the ceiling. She thought about Zoltar, about his reaction seeing the little Gnomes in their cars. It made him happy that they'd done something good, helped others the look on his face said as much.

Watching the spirits of the Pixies had given her such a feeling of accomplishment, it gave her a sense of purpose—a reason for being invited to take part in the new community. Gone were the worries that she wouldn't fit in, the question now would be how she would handle any issues that arose from integrating so many species at once. Of course, she had to worry how the students would handle the new atmosphere as well.

Interrupting her train of thought, her phone was buzzing with an alarm indicating she had just enough time to get to her next session. Scooping up her laptop bag and phone, she headed off to her next class. She studied the schedule on the tiny screen. Barb, Grace's friend, was teaching Ethics and Accounting. She was about to get a double dose of Grace's friend.

She hurried off toward the East wing, nearly missing the beginning of class as she grabbed the only seat left. Through her peripheral, she saw Zoltar studying something in front of him.

"I'm Barbara Robertson." She had her name written on the whiteboard. "Since you are my colleagues, you'll be referring to me as Barb, but I won't accept the same from my students. What I'll be teaching them aside from collegiate accounting, is ethics. We shifters have a moral code that is centered around nature and pack. The human world is very different and you fine folks are about to get a serious awakening."

Wendy pulled out her laptop and flipped it open.

"You won't be needing that," Barb said, pointing a laser pointer at Wendy. "Put it away. What I need is everyone's focus right up here."

Her face boiling with embarrassment, she quickly closed the laptop and stuffed it in her bag. Her only intention to take notes and record the session, it seemed overkill to call her out. Still, Wendy obeyed and as soon as her bag rested on the floor, her gaze rested firmly on the new professor.

"Most of you don't know that the Lycan Queen and I went to the same human college. I know she has been adamant since her arrival with regards to the rights of females. I welcome you all to Equal Opportunity and Sexual Harassment laws. The humans had something called affirmative action years ago that afforded the same rights and privileges to men and women equally." When gasps and murmurs filled the room, Barb only smiled.

"Yes, yes, welcome to the twenty-first century. Now that we are an official university and a legal employer, you'll find women hold the same station as men. No one is subservient to the other notwithstanding management roles, which we'll talk about momentarily."

She smiled as Barb laid it on thick for the males in the room. By the end of class, she could see why Grace was fond of this woman—not to mention why she was so insistent on fair treatment of the women. To her, it was normal and anything less was unconscionable. She liked the way the new world was taking shape. Words like lawsuit and jail time caused a bit of a small uproar in the class.

"All of my teaching sessions are recorded and emailed to my students daily. You will receive today's session this evening if you care to review anything you might have missed. With that, I'm happy to release you for the remainder of the day."

As Wendy headed through the door she heard Barb call her name. She flung her bag over her other shoulder and turned around.

"I'm sorry I was harsh on you. The way Grace talks about you, I know you are one hellova Lycan. Please don't think I have anything but the utmost respect for you. I just refuse to let the males see me as weak." She clutched the pen in her hand.

Wendy stared at her for a moment. Clutching the pen could be a sign of nerves. "No worries. I'm new to this technology and had no idea you could record your sessions let alone send them to my computer. I just wanted to be sure I took detailed notes. I'm a bit silly about it actually."

Barb smiled, releasing the pen, letting it fall to the desk. "Nonsense. Thoroughness is never silly. Grace said you were type 'A'."

"Type 'A'?" Clueless as to what Barb referred, she scrunched her brow.

Fanning her hand in the air, she said, "You'll cover that

in Sociology. Anyway, you're organized. I respect that." She looked at her phone. "Damn, I'm late. I'll catch you later."

She stood in awe as Barb ran in heels out of the room. She shook her head and started out of the classroom.

"Buy you a drink?"

The sudden voice caused her to jump and put her hand over her heart as if to keep it from jumping out of her chest. "Z! You scared me to death!"

He grinned and slid her bag off her shoulder, then flung it over his own. "C'mon, I have a great martini recipe I'd like to try."

Intertwining her fingers in his, she leaned her head against his arm for a brief moment. "After today, a stiff drink is just what the doctor ordered."

"You're not kidding. Would you like some good news?" He looked at her from the corner of his eye with a hint of a smirk on his lips.

"Sure, lay it on me."

"My men have finished all of the cars. There isn't one Gnome without transportation. *And*, they're finishing the ramps now." He lifted his chin a little higher.

Her cheeks pinched at the sides, her smile was so wide. "That's glorious news. I'm so happy we could do this for them. I can't imagine how hard it's been. I'm exhausted just from sitting in class and I don't have tiny little legs to carry me there."

She felt a gentle squeeze on her hand. "I never thought anything would make me feel better than the pride I felt building this school. But converting a few toy cars...of that, I think I'm the most proud."

"Really?" She pulled back from him a bit to measure his face. "Why?"

His large shoulders rose and fell. "The school is just a building. What the people do inside the building will be what really matters—what makes a difference for us all. But your idea with the cars...we solved the problem of a species that no one really appreciates."

"What? That's ludicrous. Didn't you say they ran all of the wiring for the school? That's a big task." She shook her head. She could not imagine the Gnomes work went unappreciated.

"Yes," he said with a sigh. "Haven't you noticed how most people dismiss them? Grace has been the only one to really take a knee and speak with them. Then you come along. Not only do you treat them with kindness and respect, you invited Mary on a run—something no one else had even thought of. Topping that off was the fact you had the desire to help them, to improve their situation. That's really special, Wendy."

Admittedly, helping had given her warm feelings of elation.

"Here we are," he pushed open the door to his living quarters. "Make yourself comfortable. I'll mix the drinks."

She followed him into the kitchen. "So what did you think about our last class?"

Grinning he placed her bag on the counter. "You're asking *me*?" He chuckled as he pulled liquor bottles from the cabinet.

"What do you mean, *me*? Of course *you*. Why is that so funny?" She put her hand on her hip annoyed at his laughter.

After filling a silver shaker with ice from the freezer, he started pouring liquor in. "Have you forgotten I'm a Centaur?"

"Of course not! That's not an answer." She folded her arms over her chest. "Are you being evasive? Just answer the question."

Screwing the top on the liquor bottle and turning around to face her, he leaned his behind on the counter and crossed his legs at the ankle. "We have no women, Wendy. Not to be offensive, but I always thought Lycan men were so stupid. They treat you like second class citizens unless they're bonded with you, then they grow territorial, but still don't show the level of respect I'd want if I were a woman. I believe women were meant to be by our sides, not behind us." He shrugged. "Or do you disagree?"

Her arms fell to her sides. The thought of being less had never crossed her mind, not once. She never felt like a second-class citizen, but now that more than one person had pointed it out, it made her feel angry if not a bit defensive.

"Well, not exactly. But I think you might be underestimating—"

"The first woman in power in ages, nearly gets her Alpha title stripped away because, well...she's female. Your Lycan Queen often grew angry at her King before they were mated for constantly trying to keep her in check."

"How would you know?"

"People talk, Wendy." He shook his head. "To the point, however, it took a Lycan who was raised a human to start what most of the civilized world deems normal. We think ourselves superior to humans, but they've had this figured out for a while." He took a step closer to her. "Women," he said in a low voice as he took another step, "should be cherished."

She took a step back and felt the wall against her back.

"Loved," he said in nearly a whisper, "and respected." His fingers were under her chin, though she didn't recall seeing them coming. He tilted her face up and brushed his lips against hers. "Don't you agree?"

The humming in her brain drowned out Z's words as his breath tickled her face and his lips brushed against hers. When his fingers traced her jaw bone to the back of her neck, her knees began to feel like gelatinous. Finally, when the tips of his fingers curled into her hair and pulled her against him, she was lost in the passion of the kiss. Running her hands along the length of his arms she clutched onto him when she reached his broad shoulders.

His tongued teased her lips as he pulled back. "Ready for that drink?"

"Hmm?" She blinked. "Uh, what?"

"Drinks. Remember?" He stepped back and picked up the shaker, pushed on the top and began to shake.

Weren't we talking about something? She tugged on the collar of her blouse, feeling a bit too warm. "I'll just, uh, waiting in...over there, the living room." She turned on her heel and bumped into the wall. The heat from the kiss was damned near unbearable, but the added prickle of embarrassment had her cheeks ablaze. She cursed, stepped around the wall, and darted for the living room.

I'm acting like a star-struck teenage girl. Get a grip already! She fanned herself and took a seat on the sofa, the cool faux leather offering a bit of relief. That was, until *he* came in the room carting two martini glasses. Every nerve felt raw.

"I'm sorry, but could you, um, control yourself for just a moment. I need to regroup," she asked, feeling thoroughly ashamed for the request.

"I would if I could, but I'm already firmly in control of myself, Wendy." He laughed as he placed the glasses on the table. "Perhaps I'm not the one who needs to rein things in a bit."

"Are you teasing me?" Her mouth fell slack.

"Perhaps." With a wink in her direction, he picked up a glass and handed it to her.

She sipped at the cocktail. It was a bit strong but fruity. The liquid was cool at first, then warm as it rolled down her throat and made its way into her belly. She took a big breath of air and let it out. It had the relaxing effect she was hoping for. "That's pretty delicious, but a little strong."

"Still what the doctor ordered?"

She eyed him and tightened her lips. "You always make me smile."

"Likewise." He lifted his glass in a mock toast. "Now, what I'm really wondering is if you're ready for my class tomorrow."

"I'm not ready for any of this if I'm honest. But sure, I'll enjoy a little combat training. I'm dying to know what a Centaur is going to teach a Lycan." It was her turn to tease and she wasn't going to miss out.

With a glint in his eye and a smirk on his lips, he said, "So it's like that, huh? We'll see in class."

She saw an orange glow reflecting off the television surface, she turned around to see a small campfire burning outside. "Oh I do miss the fires."

"Would you like to go?"

"Please? It's something my pack used to do several times a week. There's just something about sitting around a fire with your pack. It's really a bonding thing." She looked down at the martini glasses. "Maybe we can take something a bit more portable."

He shook his head and chuckled.

"What?"

"Nothing. How does wine sound?" He stood and held out a hand. She took it and lifted herself off of the couch.

"Good but," she picked up the martini and knocked it back, "that was too good to waste." She handed him the empty glass. "Meet you out there!" She moved quickly through the patio doors in the rear of the apartment to the courtyard outside.

"Wendy!" Tiffany stood next to Grace.

"Oh, Tiff! It's so good to see you." She hurried over to her and threw her arms around her. "How are you little girl? My gosh, you look so different." She pulled Tiffany back and eyed her. "You've lost weight."

Her shoulders rose and fell in a noncommittal shrug. "Yeah, they don't give Lycan portions at that school. Humans must eat a lot less."

Grace laughed. "Yes, I always took extra food with me to school. The food is barely enough to survive on. Sorry, I forgot to say something."

"Here's your wine," Zoltar joined them handing her a

glass.

"Uh, Tiffany, Zoltar," Wendy waved back and forth.

Tiffany elbowed her and grinned. "How could I forget the Centaur King? Very nice to see you again."

"Likewise." He nodded and after a quick glance at Wendy, left to take a seat by the fire.

Tiffany leaned in and whispered. "So you and the king, eh? Nice!" She giggled. "Sorry, I've been sipping whiskey for the last hour—good Lycan whiskey too."

Placing her free arm around her, she gave her another squeeze. "I'm so happy you're here. It's nice to have another familiar face."

Tiffany nodded and Wendy followed her over to the fire, sitting next to Zoltar.

"Really magnificent, you two!" Grace beamed. Her face lit by the fire and whatever she'd been drinking.

Roman put his arm around her as he sat down. "I think my wife is talking about the cars for the Gnomes."

"Not just that. Wendy, the dancing…nice. Very nice, indeed." Grace raised her glass.

Desperate for a change in attention, she scrambled to find another topic. "I really like the courtyard. It's such a wonderful touch of home."

"This is for the staff only. The students' dorms are not connected so we can have a bit of comradery out here." Zoltar nudged her. "You know, for strengthening the pack."

"How is that coming along?" Tiffany chimed in.

Everyone glanced around.

Grace smiled and blinked heavy lids. "Slow. But it'll happen."

There was an uneasy silence that lasted a few moments. Wendy worried about the others and their doubts about forming an integrated pack. It wasn't that she didn't share those doubts so much as she wanted to overcome them.

"I think we're making headway. Don't you?" Zoltar whispered.

She leaned against him, feeling his warmth ooze into her. "Baby steps." She took a sip of wine, enjoying the earthiness and warmth of it. Then she felt the overwhelming urge come over her—Zoltar had finally released his hold.

Grace and Tiffany both looked at him with their mouths open.

"Sorry, I need to relax for a few moments." He stood to leave.

Roman jumped out of his seat. "Sit down, Z. The girls will have to control themselves." He glanced at Grace and Tiffany. "Or is that not possible?"

Grace giggled. Tiffany followed.

"We're fine," Grace said leaning into Roman. "I have you after all."

Rolling her eyes, Tiffany waved her hands as if to shoo him away. "Just, uh, stay on your side of the fire."

Wendy smiled up at him and patted the bench next to her. "Yeah, keep it over here, you filthy Centaur."

An outburst of laughter from Grace was quickly contagious as it spread around the fire.

He smiled at her and reclaimed his seat. "Yes, ma'am." He pulled the bottle around to fill her glass. "We probably should eat something."

"Over there," Tiffany pointed to a table in the corner. "I brought deep dish pizza."

With a pat to his stomach, he grinned. "I thought I smelled sausage."

"I'll get it. Just relax." Wendy giggled. She shook her head. The martini must have been stronger than she thought. She was feeling giddy.

After pizza and the remainder of the wine, Grace, Tiffany, and Roman left the campfire.

"You know, I saw this," Zoltar took the glass out of her hand. "I saw you and me by this fire in a vision. I didn't know what it meant but now that it's come to fruition, I couldn't be happier."

Her mouth fell slack.

EIGHT

Disbelief washed over him. He was sitting by the fire with the woman he'd been falling for. She'd been receptive, even eager to spend time with him. Fear and regret had plagued him after running out the morning after their first lovemaking session. Treating her like a fling was not in his repertoire.

But here, the orange glow of the fire illuminated her beautiful face and her silky blonde hair. Every time she smiled he melted inside. He'd never thought a mate to be a possibility, yet here she was, a potential interested mate.

He listened to her talk about their classes, her excitement and trepidation. Her dancing eyes were wild as she spoke about the possibilities of their future. Her full lips moving so quickly, he fought not to still them with his own. Wendy was perfect in every way. How could he keep from rushing things when all he wanted to do was experience the bond he'd heard about so many times before? Longing to be so connected with someone, someone special, like the beautiful Lycan before him—so full of compassion for others.

"It's getting late. We should douse the fire and turn in."

She stood looking around. "Ah, a bucket of water." She picked it up and poured it on the logs.

He silently punished himself for not taking care of it for her. "After you," he said in an attempt to reclaim some chivalry. He'd fought hard to maintain control by the fire, but had been overcome with pride looking at her, he'd nearly cried.

Following her through the sliding glass doors, he knew he'd have to make a choice and quickly. Did he pursue another moment of intimacy with her, or let her go to her own place alone?

Delightfully, the choice had been made for him, when she took a sharp left turn toward the bedroom rather than walk to the front door.

"Am I being presumptuous?" she asked with a grin.

He crossed the threshold into the bedroom and scooped her up in his arms. "You're taking a very difficult choice out of my hands." He crushed her lips with his, eager to feel her silky skin against him; to feel her soft folds accepting—enveloping him. After carefully carrying her to the bed, he released her from his kiss long enough to rip his shirt over his head.

"I could get used to this," she cooed as he kissed the length of her neck.

That's what I'm hoping for!

Her warm hands ran the length of his arms before strong fingers curled into the flesh on his back. The pressure in his pants grew increasingly uncomfortable. He reached down and popped the button and unzipped himself, freeing his throbbing cock from captivity.

Running his hand from her ankle, he massaged his way up to her hips, and then unbuttoned her as well. He curled his fingers around the waistband and gave them a gentle tug, slowly pulling her pants down under her bottom, over the peaks of her knees and down to her ankles.

She kicked them off to the side and pulled at his arms. "Please," she panted, "I love foreplay, but please, just…take me this time."

He could feel the lascivious grin spread across his face, all too willing to obey and satisfy her needs. He had teased her mercilessly the first time and figured he owed her an easier time or three. Crawling up a bit, he eased himself between her legs, resting his elbows on each side of her. He brushed his lips against her, feeling her pant of need.

She was already wet and wanting. He pressed his lips on hers as he entered her, reveling in the sound of her moaning into his mouth. The slick warmth coaxed his cock as he retreated slightly and pushed into her once more. Fighting the urge to fuck her with everything he had, he kept the rhythm slow to enjoy the exquisite creature pushing against him from below.

Her hands pulled at his bottom, silently begging for more as she moaned with each stroke. He felt her calves roll onto his hips, willing him to go deeper. He pushed into her with his entirety and she gasped, her eyes closed tight. He remained there momentarily as he peppered her jaw line with kisses. He laced his fingers above her head and pushed into her again, feeling her inner walks clenching around his cock. Her body responding to the short hard thrusts calling for more.

"Ohhh," she moaned again, pulling, clawing at his back.

He kept his slow firm pace with her and watched her face with each thrust as she pushed her head against the bed, tilting her jaw up. Her throat was utterly exposed. Every piece of literature he'd read told him this was an offering of a bond.

"Bond. Take it! Take it!"

He froze for a split second, taken aback by the voice inside his head. It was only the second time he'd heard it.

When she opened her eyes, they were ablaze, golden glow illuminating her face. Her body clenched around him as her orgasm overwhelmed her.

Her face had morphed and her fangs had elongated.

She trembled beneath him. "Oh God, I'm sorry. I'm sorry. I didn't bite you. Did I bite?" Her hand shook over her mouth.

"It's okay. Nothing happened." He kissed her forehead for reassurance. His heart fell, realizing her body had taken over her free will. She wasn't so much offering a bond as her wolf was trying to do it for her.

Rolling off, he lay facing her, inspecting her emotional state. "Are you okay?"

Breathing hard, and then swallowing, she gasped before she spoke. "I don't know what came over me. I almost…I almost bit you." She felt her face once more and appeared to be relieved her fangs were gone. "It was the orgasm, I think." Her fangs had retreated as she calmed.

She looked down, noting he hadn't climaxed and pushed him to his back. He watched her move to her knees between his legs. She smiled up at him before taking him into her mouth.

He dropped his head on the pillow and closed his eyes. Her delicious lips were now wrapped around his cock. Using her hand, she pumped the shaft while licking and sucking the top. His thighs tightened as he fought the urge to thrust himself down her throat. He watched her work him, felt her moaning onto his cock. It was more than he could take. The pressure released as his orgasm washed over him, forcing his seed into her mouth.

Gelatinous goo was his body. He'd been reduced to a pile of withered Centaur, his woman pulling every drop from him.

She excused herself to the bathroom and he could not help but admire her naked backside as she left the room, her perfect ass, each cheek moving with the extension and retraction of each step. A wide admiring grin pulled at his lips.

He closed his eyes, relaxed into a state of contentment he'd never thought possible. His woman wanted him. If he was patient, maybe, just maybe, they could make it permanent. What would bonding with her entail? It seemed impossible to want her any more than he did now.

Boom! Rumble...rumble. Boom! Loud explosions rocked the building.

He leaped from the bed, snatching up his pants.

She ran into the room, her mouth open, her hands over her chest, horror painted on her face. "What the hell was that?"

"Get dressed. Quickly!" He tossed her pants to her then yanked his shirt over his head.

Boom!

"Dear God! We are under attack!" Tears glistened in her eye and she pulled her shoes on.

He laced his boots, frantic to protect the school he'd built. "Stay by me," he ordered as he grabbed her by the wrist and pulled her to the entryway. He looked her in the eye, seeing only fear. "I won't let anything happen to you."

She nodded.

He pulled her into the hall, and ran toward the screams. He could hear the crackling of fire, smelled the smoke and sulfur. His heart thundered in his chest, his vision blurred as he looked around frantic and angry. Theron skidded to a halt in front of him and handed him a bow and bag of arrows.

"They're outside!" Theron yelled.

*

Wendy couldn't focus on one solitary thing as she ran with Zoltar toward the entry. There was so much chaos, the stench of fear and smoke overwhelming her senses. Their school had been attacked. *Why? Why would someone do this?*

When they reached the door, Z shifted. She shifted to wolf, ready to defend her home...her pack. She spotted Grace and Roman, their enormous wolves chasing down smaller wolves.

"There!" Z dug his hooves in and took off toward the East wing where two human forms had some sort of large gun pointed at the building.

She snarled, curling her claws to get better traction as she launched in their direction. She sprinted, stretching her legs as far and as fast as they would carry her. She tested the air with her nose. The men were Lycan, but not anyone she knew. She caught Zoltar out the corner of her eye pull back on his bow. He aimed toward the one on the left. She darted right and leaped. The man shifted to his wolf form a split second before she connected. She latched on to the back of his neck and pulled hard as her paws connected with the earth. The move had rolled the wolf hard onto his back. Before he could scramble to his feet, she latched onto his throat.

The wolf froze.

She considered her options as she tightened her grip on the wolf's throat. She could feel his heartbeat racing in her mouth. A little more pressure and she could rip his throat out. But she wanted answers. A dead Lycan couldn't answer questions. Maintaining her hold on him, she shifted her gaze around. Z and Theron had taken each flank, standing over her, bows drawn, but away…guarding and protecting her.

"Good," she heard Grace in her mind. *"You kept him alive. Let's find out what these bastards are after."*

She saw Grace approach in her human form and touch the wolf. The air around him shimmered as he shifted from her touch.

Wendy growled and kept her grip on the man's throat until Grace patted her shoulder. She released him, stepped back, and shifted. She turned and looked at the school, which was remarkably still intact. Some of the wooden accents had burned and the side of the building was scorched, but the walls stood. The school was going to be okay. She breathed a sigh of relief.

"Speak!" Zoltar boomed as he placed a hoof between

the man's legs.

The man looked down at his crotch and the hoof pressing down on it. "You filthy pigs!" He spat.

Zoltar pressed a little harder.

Grace knelt down and stared the man in the face. "You will tell me why." Her eyes burned violet, illuminating his face and the ground around him.

His jaw fell slack as he stared into her eyes. He started to shake. "No!"

Roman shifted mid run and stopped short of running over Grace.

"Separatists?" Grace shook her head and stood.

"What?" Wendy asked. "What the hell are Separatists?"

Grace looked at Roman. They must have communicated something telepathically because they both nodded in understanding.

Roman patted Zoltar on his shoulder. "Take this piece of shit to the basement and lock him up in a closet. Then I want all of the royalty and you, Wendy," he said nodding in her direction, "to meet in the conference room next to Grace's office."

Grace turned to Theron. "Please see if the Fae can help with the smoke. Let's salvage what wood we can on the exterior. Then get your men on examining the structure. I want to be sure it's safe. I have Tiffany on triage."

They all nodded, anger still painted on everyone's face.

"I'll go with you, Z, to keep this asshole in check." She grabbed the man by his collar and jerked him to his feet. "Give me one reason, just one, to rip out your throat!" *If you hurt one member of my pack and I'll have your ass!* She jerked back, shocked that she'd considered them all her pack.

Zoltar shifted to his human form and grabbed the man under the arm. She kept her grip firm, but had to follow him as she had no idea how to get to the basement or where they intended on keeping the cretin.

Tears stung her eyes as the smoke in the building assaulted her. She saw Gnomes, whizzing by in their cars, which were loaded down with medical supplies.

"Wendy!" Mary skidded to a halt and jumped out of her car. "You're okay!"

"I'm so glad to see you're okay, Mary. I'll check on you later. Be very careful, there are a lot of folks running around."

Mary hugged Wendy's shin again and hurried back to her car. *Yes. My pack!* She growled at the man.

Zoltar moved with such swiftness and purpose, she had to walk fairly fast to keep up. They rounded a corner at the end of a hall and descended the stairs. She'd not seen this part of the castle before. The temperature dropped as they headed below ground.

At the bottom of the stairs, he flipped a switch on the wall and the basement illuminated. He jerked the man's arm so hard, she lost her grip on the other. For a second, she was worried the Lycan would shift and run, having the clear advantage on the stone floors. He didn't shift. He didn't run. Instead he looked at Zoltar in horror.

"What are you going to do to me?" he sniveled.

With one large step toward a wall, he slammed the man into it. "I should kill you. I should rip off your arms and beat you to death with them for harming innocent creatures. But I'm not." He squeezed his eyes shut tight for a second. "I'm going to lock you in a room while I go discuss your fate with the others. Personally, I'd like to skin you and let the Gnomes make coats out of your fur. If one of them even has a scratch…that may very well be your fate!"

The thought of Lycan fur being used as a coat should have horrified her, but the idea actually appealed to her—as penance for harming her family.

He grabbed the man by the hair and pulled him three feet to a door. He jerked the door open and put the man in the opening. He partially shifted, so he had one back leg of his horse, spun and kicked the guy to the back of the room, then slammed the door shut before resuming human form. After testing the door to be sure it was locked, he took a deep breath. "I'm sorry you had to see that."

With her hands firmly on her hips, she gasped. "Well I nearly ripped his throat out, so don't apologize to me. Come on. Let's go see Grace and the others."

He took her hand in his and led her up the stairs. She felt a bit numb as she'd been overwhelmed with anger, concern, and fear. This was the second time something tragic happened after making love to him. She'd have a tiny moment of happiness before something horrifying took place. The bombing had scared her, made her feel panic like she'd never felt. She was concerned about everyone she was getting to know, and those she'd yet to meet.

The poor Pixies had barely recovered from their loss.

Things seemed to have quieted down when they reached the top of the stairs. People moved swiftly about, but didn't look as panicked or fear-stricken. Most of the shifters remained in animal form, feeling more apt to handle themselves in their stronger form. The Fae all had eyes burning blue with anger. They may not have glowed like Lycan eyes, but they were burning and fierce. Her heart gave a little start. She'd never seen an angry Fae. They were intimidating.

His grip was firm but not crushing as they ascended the final flight of stairs and made their way into the conference room.

The first sight upon entering the room was of Beauregard, King of the Fae, standing with his arms folded over his chest. He was a mountain of a man and towered over Zoltar, who stood almost six and a half feet tall. His eyes burned with the same crystal blue hue as the other Fae she'd passed. Standing next to him, tapping his axe against his hand was Oden, King of the Dwarves and his mate, Lela the Queen. Her short, squat, four foot frame matched her mate's. Her raven curly hair a mess, framed a face blackened by soot and streaked with tears.

Ella, the Pixie Queen, might have looked the most demonic. She was so furious her eyes, normally ocean blue, were blood red with a tiny black dot in the center. Wendy had never seen an angry Pixie and seeing Ella with eyes that looked like pools of blood was unsettling. The woman vibrated as she tried to wait for the others.

Roman and Grace entered the room; both had the same scowl, furrowed brow, tightened jaws.

"The Lycan Wendy managed to hold had some useful information that sheds some light on the violence we've experienced." Roman scratched his jaw. "It seems Grace's plan to integrate us all and bring peace has caused uproar among some packs," he looked at Grace and took her hand and his, "and not just Lycan packs."

Grace gave Roman's hand a squeeze and took a seat. Wendy followed suit, her knees buckling as the thought of more violence weakened her.

The others followed suit and took seats around the conference table. Zoltar sat next to her, putting a protective arm on the back of her chair.

"I looked into his mind." Grace shook her head as a tear spilled down her cheek. "The Pixie murdered in the woods was step one of their plan to rip us apart. The bombing of the school was intended to scare students and our human professors away." She took a deep breath. "They're calling themselves Separatists because they believe all species should be separated. Their biggest fear is inter-breeding and thinning out the bloodlines." She cleared her throat and shot a quick glance at Wendy then resumed addressing everyone.

"There is a plan to murder one of my Lycans for fraternizing with a male of another species." She pounded her fist on the table. "I will *not* allow them to succeed."

She knew. She knew it was her. The plan to murder a Lycan was a hit on her, because of Zoltar. Everyone around the table pounded their fists against the surface,

Wendy included. She was a *Lycan* and she was not going down without a fight. Others had often seen her as meek and mild mannered. Most didn't know she fought in the last war, just a young adult at the time, or that she'd been trained by Tom, head of the Belfast pack's security.

She'd put the past behind her. Her days of bloodshed had haunted her for nearly forty years. They were in for a surprise if they thought she'd lay there and take it. She *would* fight. She would love who *she* wanted.

"It's me, isn't it Grace?" When she spoke, she did so in a low, even voice.

Grace nodded, her mouth turned down in concern. "Don't worry. We'll protect you."

"Let them come."

"What? No." Zoltar looked at her, his eyes wide.

"You're the combat tactics professor *and* my mate. They want a fight—they'll *get* one!" She growled. The reflection of her glowing eyes illuminating his face. Adrenaline soared through her veins causing tiny vibrations in her extremities.

"Mate? When did that happen?" Tiffany asked as she entered the room.

Wendy spun around in her chair. "Tiffany! You're okay!" She leaped from her chair and hugged her.

Mary's car skidded into the room. "Hey! Wait!" She jumped out of her car and ran to Wendy.

She picked her up and placed her on the table top before reclaiming her seat.

Beauregard stood and leaned over, his knuckles on the table. "I know we wanted to wait. I know we wanted to take time to form a law enforcement branch and a government. But we need to put a tactical team together now. We need to hunt these vermin in their den and decimate them." He flexed the long, lean muscles of his arms. "We can make changes as necessary, but this threat needs to be eradicated."

Everyone banged on the table again. Ella placed her

hand on his bicep. "We are really talented at reading auras. I have one man in mind for the job, if you'll allow it. He can help assemble your team and his particular talents would also help you spot someone with a guilty conscience."

"That'd be fine by me."

Roman stood to command attention. "I don't think any of us have objections to you heading this new, uh, department, Beauregard."

Zoltar stood, Wendy shooting up next to him. "You can have as many of my men as you see fit. They're at your service."

Lela climbed on top of her chair. "All my people are fierce warriors. You may elect any of them to serve your cause."

Mary stood and put her hands on her hips. "Listen, we don't have leaders, but since I'm the first to make a true friend here, the Gnomes have asked me to speak on their behalf. I know we're little. I know we can't move as fast, nor can we fight like you. But we do have stealth on our side, and we are excellent climbers. We can sneak into places you can't. We can hear better than any of you. You should take one of us with you. We can help." She lifted her chin.

Beauregard smiled down at her. "Of course. It would be an honor to have one of you with us. We're all in this together. We all have strengths and weaknesses. This is *our* pack now."

Ella's eyes had calmed to their normal blue shade. "Mary, I'll have Grant, one of my Pixies, read your auras to find the fiercest among you. Would that be suitable?"

Wendy's bottom lip quivered. Everyone in the room showed so much respect toward one another. Species that had mistrusted each other in the past, coming together, truly. It touched her deeply. It wasn't only possible for the different species to form an honest-to-goodness pack—it happened in front of her eyes.

"Tiffany," Grace's voice was low, solemn. "Please fill us in on the damage."

She stepped forward slowly and placed her palms on the table. "There were many injuries, but thankfully, most of us heal fairly quickly. One of the Dwarves died from falling down the stairs when the first bomb hit. She just...um," tears spilled over her eyes and ran down her face. "She broke her neck. One of the Fae tried to heal her but it was too late." She looked at Lela and Oden. "I'm very sorry."

Beauregard bowed his head and whispered silently with his eyes closed as if in prayer. Oden and Lela pounded their chests twice and said something in their native tongue Wendy didn't recognize.

"Ella, you have two in the infirmary. They're using your brand of magic to heal, so there really wasn't anything for me to do. None of the Gnomes were injured beyond bumps and scrapes. Other than that, everyone seems to be okay." She shook her head. "Honestly, this castle is so durable it was the shockwave of the blast that did the most damage to the people inside."

Wendy grabbed Zoltar's hand and gave it a squeeze. "I know what our moral code says about interrogation." She cleared her throat. She looked at Roman and Grace and furrowed her brow. "But can you two dig in our hostage's head and find a location of where these Separatists hide?"

Roman jutted his chin at Zoltar. "I think *we* should go. You up for it?"

"Absolutely." He puffed out his chest.

"I'm going too." Ella's voice cracked. "He killed one of mine and I want answers!" She crossed her arms over her tiny frame.

"Don't kill him," Grace said as she wagged her finger. "Not yet."

"Not a problem." He looked at the Fae King. "Put a team together. We'll give you all of the information as soon as we have it."

Zoltar leaned over and whispered in Wendy's ear. "I'd like to discuss this *mate* idea when I return. Be safe." He kissed her cheek.

She leaned against his kiss, feeling warmth and a sense of calm ooze into her.

Everyone filed out of the room. Everyone except for Grace, Tiffany, and Wendy. The three moved in closer to each other. Grace threw her arms around them both and pulled them in. "Oh girls, I'm so relieved you're both okay."

"Let's talk about this mate thing now!" Tiffany squeaked.

If she wasn't so spent from the evening's ordeal she probably would have blushed. "I don't know what to say. I just feel...at ease with him. It feels natural, like it's always been."

A smirk spread across Grace's face. "That's how I felt with Roman. He seemed familiar from the beginning, like it was just, normal to be with him. Like no one else could suit me better."

"But it's put a target on my back." Wendy's shoulders fell. "Honestly, I just wanted to, be a bit more than friends because I didn't know if I'd still be accepted."

"Of course! Don't be dense. This is a new pack—an integrated pack. Roman and I only want to see you happy. Honestly, I'm glad you have your cookies and milk." A wicked grin spread across Grace's face as she wiggled an eyebrow.

"Oh Grace. Poor form." She gave her a weak smile.

Tiffany scratched her head. "Cookies and milk?"

"Oh yeah, Wendy couldn't figure out whether to strip him naked or dunk him in milk and eat him up." Grace laughed and winked at her.

Placing a palm on her forehead, she tried to cool her embarrassment. "Ya' just had to share that, didn't you?" If she were honest with herself, she was grateful for the humor. "This   is   so   inappropriate,   given   the circumstances."

Theron jogged into the room. "Sorry, where's Zoltar?"

"Interrogating someone. What's up?" Grace asked.

He smiled, apparently pleased at the thought of interrogation. "The building is still structurally sound. The Pixies with their ability to fly around are scrubbing the upper floors on the exterior, removing the soot. We should have this place like new before the students arrive. Your vampire has brought a witch with him. She's casting protective charms around the perimeter of the property. Everyone okay?"

"One Dwarf lost, some other injuries but that seems to be the extent of it." Tiffany shifted her weight and tucked a strand of hair behind her ear.

"Oh," His eyes widened. "Uh, sorry."

Wendy sniffed. Theron hadn't had control over himself and Tiffany was reacting.

Wait! Why didn't I notice immediately?

"Because you claimed a mate." Grace spoke in her head. *"We can still scent it, but the effect isn't as strong."*

Receiving Grace's thought she looked at her Queen who had a large smile plastered on her face.

"It's a very powerful thing. Your wolf must be very serious about him to prevent you from picking up on Theron's scent."

She rolled her eyes. If her wolf had her way, they'd have been bonded their first time alone together. "Thank you, Theron. I'll let Z know."

He nodded at her before turning to give Tiffany a wink then spun on his heel making his exit.

"Down girl." Grace whispered in the young Lycan's ear.

Tiffany spun around fanning her blazing red face. "Holy hotness!"

"Ladies, we're in crisis mode here. Focus!" She chuckled.

With a wink at her, Grace turned and smiled. "Tiff, can you give us a moment. Go get cleaned up and try to get some rest."

She nodded and waved as she left the room.

Turning to face her, Grace motioned to a chair. "Have a seat."

Swallowing hard, she pulled out a chair and planted her bottom in it.

"In case this was a point of concern, the ancestors tell me that you can have a Lycan bond with Zoltar." Grace flattened her palms against the surface of the table. "You know, if that is a concern."

She waved a dismissive hand in the air. "Well yeah, he's part Lycan."

The open mouth of the Lycan Queen displayed her shock. "Oh." Grace leaned back in her chair. "Oh!" Her brow furrowed.

She enjoyed watching Grace as she digested the information. "Yeah."

"Wait. Why don't I smell it on him?" Grace stared at the table, looking like she was searching her mind for something. "He doesn't spend much time in Lycan form. Does he?"

She shook her head. "No. He says Centaur is his true form that he has to force the human transition, and Lycan is even that much further for him to go." She cleared her throat. "His wolf is large like yours, but out of shape."

Grace nodded, her eyes squinting in concentration. "Because he doesn't spend much time with the beast. Interesting. Well," she pulled her hair back from her face, "no matter. If he is your mate, he is your mate. No one else's feelings on the issue matter. You have all of our support. There hasn't been a Centaur Queen since ancient times so you'd be the first."

"What? No. I'm not royalty. I'm just a Lycan...an average one at that."

Grace burst into laughter. "So was Roman, until we bonded. And you're hardly average." She leaned toward her, invading her space. "Pull up your bootstraps. Things change when that happens and not like a normal Lycan bonding. It's special…powerful. You both will acquire abilities you never thought possible."

She hadn't notice Grace take her hand, so she was a bit startled when she felt her squeeze. "It'll be nice having another woman who understands what I'm going through, what I experience. The worst part is feeling so protective over creatures who barely know you. And…you saw how I reacted to the murdered Pixie. I'm sorry." She released her hand. "I'm probably scaring you. It's wonderful and glorious most of the time. You may lose contact with your wolf for a short time as she goes through a transformation, but mine assured me she was fine. The howling is just confusion."

She gulped and her heart thundered in her chest. She'd just a few moments ago, claimed Z as hers, without his input though, she was fairly certain he felt the same about her. She hadn't thought about becoming a Queen. The very thought worried her. Royalty? What would happen to her? Howling? Losing her wolf? She fell back in her chair. "I should go get cleaned up."

Ready to put some distance between them, she shoved off the chair and shuffled back toward her room. The noise and chaos from earlier had settled into workers cleaning, and the clacking of Centaur hooves in the halls.

"Wendy?" She heard her name and looked around.

"Down here," the tiny voice said.

She looked down to see Mary standing next to her little car.

"I'm sorry. I'm in a bit of a fog. Are you okay?" She took to her knee.

"My stupid car. Not stupid. It's not stupid." The tiny woman started to cry. "But the batteries are both dead because they weren't done charging when everything happened and…"

She gave a soft smile. "Don't cry." She held out hand and nudged Mary's little cheek to dry her tear. "I'll give you a lift."

The tiny woman wiped her face and looked at her shoes. "Can I confess, I'm a bit scared?"

"Me too, my friend. Listen, how about you stay with me tonight? How does that sound? We can keep each other company. Heck, I can even make some popcorn. Do you like popcorn?"

She smiled up at her host. "I love popcorn."

"Good! Let's just take your car back to your place so you can charge the batteries. Grab some night clothes and I'll give you a lift back to my place." The air around her shimmered as she shifted.

Climbing on her back, the little Gnome giggled. "This will never get old."

She picked up the car with her teeth, taking care not to damage the plastic and trotted off to the West wing. As she passed each hall she looked over her shoulder to see if Mary acknowledged her hall. By the third, she felt a tiny pat on her head. "This one, all the way to the end."

Halting at the last door, she squatted down, allowing her passenger to hop off of her back. When she eased the car out of her mouth and onto the floor, she used her snout to push it toward the door. Mary opened the door and pulled on the front of the car until it was inside. She lifted the battery out of the back and set it in the charging dock.

"Two seconds. I'll be right back." Mary left the door open and skipped out of sight.

Peeking inside, she could see that it was a miniature replica of her own home, built to size for the little Gnomes. More appreciation for Zoltar flooded her heart. The man had really thought of everything. She gave a little snort when she pictured the Centaurs, with their big hands, trying to assemble the small cabinets that were about the size of a five gallon bucket. "I'm back!" She had a tiny backpack slung over her shoulders.

Mary closed the door behind her and climbed on her

back. She waited until she felt a firm tug on her fur, a reaffirmation that her new friend had a firm grip. She took off at a fast trot, hearing giggling coming from the guest on her back.

"I love this so much. Can we go faster?"

Her lips pulled up over her teeth in a wolfy grin. She took off at a dead run toward her hall, though she'd never taken the back hall to get there. She looked up at the carvings until she saw "X" carved in stone. It was her hall. She skidded to a halt and gasped. Roman and Zoltar were in the hall; both of them had what appeared to be blood on them. She ran up to them sniffing.

"It's not our blood." Zoltar knelt down. "We're fine. He's just a bleeder. Roman punched him and his nose sort of just…exploded." He looked at Mary. "You okay?"

"I'm staying with Wendy. She's making popcorn. Maybe we'll watch a movie. But yes. I'm fine now that I don't have to stay alone tonight."

"That's a great idea." He looked at Wendy. "I'll, uh, talk to you tomorrow. Can I join you ladies for coffee?"

Wendy nodded her snout up and down. She leaned her head against his leg and rubbed against him as she walked by. As much as she loved seeing him, witnessing him covered in blood was unsettling. She wanted and desperately needed a shower herself. When she reached her door, she squatted down. As soon as her little friend was safely off of her, she shifted and then opened the door.

"Wow, it looks just like mine!" The little woman's open mouth, blanketed by her hand, let out a gasp.

Once inside, she led her guest to the bathroom and filled the sink with warm water, placing Mary on the sink and closing the door to give her some privacy. She kicked off her shoes and retrieved some clean pajamas for the evening.

She looked at herself in the mirror and was shocked at her appearance. Her blonde hair looked like ash and was in a giant tangle, soot smudged on her face. She looked a mess.

"I'm all done!" Mary called from the bathroom.

She went in and scooped her up, taking her to the living room and placing her on the couch. She put the remote next to her. "See if you can't find something funny. I can't handle any more drama today."

"No kidding!" Mary pushed on the button with both hands.

She hurried off, grabbed her pajamas and took a quick shower. By the time she made it to the living room Mary had settled on a movie and had it paused.

"Let me get the popcorn made and I'll be right back."

With a grin, her head bobbed.

She hurried into the kitchen and within a few moments came back carting a big bowl of popcorn, a small measuring cup, and a shot glass. She held up the shot glass. "Is this small enough?"

She nodded. "Yep, that's what I have at my place. I found a funny movie about killing your boss."

Murder. Excellent. She forced a smile anyway.

"It's a comedy. I promise. I watched the commercials."

She scooped a few kernels of popcorn into the measuring cup and put it next to Mary, and then popped open a can of cola, filling the shot glass first.

The movie made them both laugh but by the end, Wendy could hardly keep her eyes open.

"I didn't even consider where you'd sleep," she confessed.

"Does your night stand have a drawer?" Mary stood on the couch looking up at her with large, hopeful eyes.

"Yeah?" She furrowed her brow. Having a tiny friend turned out to be quite the challenge.

"If you put one of your towels in the drawer, it'll be the perfect size for me."

Mary climbed up and sat on the bed as Wendy cleared the drawer and placed two towels inside, one to lie on and one to cover. It seemed like such a haphazard bed for her friend. It was hard not to look at such a tiny person and see her as a child. She was roughly the height of a newborn baby, but built like a woman. Though she wasn't a child, Wendy just couldn't help but feel like this bed wouldn't serve a child, let alone an adult being.

"Why the sad face?" She crossed her tiny arms over her chest.

Sitting slowly so as not to upend her friend, she folded her hands in her lap. "Please don't take offense, but I was just thinking a drawer isn't fit for someone to sleep in, not even an infant. Then..." she shrugged, her bottom lip protruding, "I sort of felt bad for equating you with an infant."

A tiny giggle filled the room. "You're funny. You really don't know much about us. That drawer is nicer than anything I slept in before coming to this school."

She studied the little woman, whose face bore seriousness despite her laughter. "And way back before we went into hiding, we often faced captivity by infertile human women. They'd keep us as pets or force us to act as if we were their children. Most of us dig out underground homes but still...we can't even make a fire without drawing attention, which means a lot of us freeze to death unless we move farther south. Even then, we have to worry about being eaten by snakes and other predators. So *that* drawer...*that* drawer that has you so concerned about me. Well *that's* going to feel like heaven. I will sleep just fine because it's warm. It's safe. It's dry and clean." Mary shuffled to her feet, walked over and kissed her on the cheek. "But it's sweet of you to be concerned."

She kissed the little woman on the forehead before picking her up and placing her, gently, in the drawer, leaving it hang open. "Maybe with integration, you can have your own villages with other shifters. I know Belfast has plenty of land. The new Alpha there seems stern but kind. She's a warrior, don't get me wrong. But she's been kind and thoughtful so far."

The little one yawned and stretched out in the drawer, propping her feet up on the drawer edge. She pulled the towel up over her shoulders. "I'm so glad we're friends. Good night."

Wendy rolled so her back was to her guest and picked at her pillow. Fact was it was nearly morning and time to get up. Physically, she was exhausted but could not imagine getting any sleep.

When Grace brought up an integrated school, she was one of the naysayers. She didn't think integration would happen, nor would it be a wise idea. But now…anything else seemed absurd. Why shouldn't they get along? What reason would there be to stay separate other than to propagate fear and mistrust?

She had grown fond of her petite new friend. The thought of something horrible happening…flying debris that would just bruise her could kill a Gnome. Logically, she knew they weren't children, but couldn't help the same feelings mothers have over their pups. These little gems should be protected. They were at the greatest risk of being hurt during an attack. The thought sickened her.

Zoltar. She had blurted out that he was her mate. She knew her feelings for him were growing. She admired his skills and that admiration only grew when he was kind to the smaller, more defenseless among them. She nearly always had butterflies in her stomach when she thought of him. But *mate* is a strong word. That is a huge commitment. Her wolf seemed to want him, whether or not he was Centaur.

But it was love. After seventy-five years of not having love, she knew this had to be it. He respected her fighting skills, not trying to hover over her, but allowing her to fight side-by-side with him to defend their home. He was kind and considerate, yet didn't treat her like a delicate flower. Their first time together was anything but average.

Solidifying the bond meant she'd be taking on

responsibility to more than just her mate. Being the wife of a royal carried a title and a heavy burden, like a crown too heavy for her head.

But she was tired of letting life occur. It was time for a change. It was *her* time. Time to take charge of *her life* and she would make *life happen* instead of letting it *happen to her*.

NINE

When sleep didn't come, Wendy got to work. She had her study materials out, those she hadn't left at Zoltar's and reviewed everything she'd received the prior day. She took a shower and crept into the bedroom to change, so as to not wake her guest, she took the clothing into the bathroom with her.

Dressed and ready for the day, she brewed a pot of coffee and whipped up some flapjacks. A gentle knock at the door caused a pull at her lips. She hurried to the door, cracked it open, and upon seeing Zoltar, flung it wide. "Coffee?" She winked and kissed him on the cheek.

"That sounds wonderful." He put an arm around her and squeezed. He swung his other arm around handing her the bag she'd left at his place.

Mary padded out to the kitchen. "Breakfast smells wonderful."

"Good morning!" He scooped her up and put her on his shoulder. "Did you two get any rest?"

"I couldn't sleep," Wendy confessed with a shrug. She began dishing the flapjacks onto plates then carried them to the table. She'd piled books on a chair so Mary could reach her plate and shooed them into the dining area.

"These are delicious," he said as he wiped his mouth with a cloth.

Mary tore pieces off and dunked them in a ramekin of syrup. "I've never had anything like it. It's really yummy!"

She shook her head, not wanting to imagine the sort of food the gnomes had to scrape together. "So, Z, I was thinking…"

Placing his fork on the table, he gave her his full attention. Beneath the blond curls resting on his forehead, he peeked out at her with the sincerest of gazes.

She blinked to regain her composure. "Mary was telling me how they've had to live, in hiding, underground, living just like rodents. It's really disgusting. I want to approach some of the shifters to see if they would accept them. They're very clever and can pull their own weight. They just need a safe place and the ability to erect real homes."

"That would be lovely!" Mary put her hands on her chest, tears glimmering in her eyes. "If they would have us, we could help. We could help them with things to earn our place. If they didn't want to accept us in their packs, well, maybe we could just…"

She scrunched her face, searching for the words.

"Coexist." He smiled at her. "I'm sure your people have skills to offer. It would be a bartering situation. That's a lovely thought."

Wendy held up her hands. "I need to find packs that are open to the idea. This isn't going to happen overnight. Mary, it would be helpful if you could meet with the others, get together a list of things you have to offer, skills and whatnot."

After clapping with excitement, she hopped off her books and used the leg of the chair to scale down to the floor. "Can you open the door for me?"

"Sure." She stood from her chair. "Done with breakfast so soon?"

"It was wonderful, but I'm too excited to eat anymore.

I really need to go." She hopped up and down.

"But, I gave you a ride here. Won't you need a lift back?" She walked with Mary to the door and opened it.

"Nope. I'll catch up with someone. Xander has given me a ride before. I think more Lycans are getting used to the idea seeing you give me a ride." She darted into the hall. "Bye!"

With a chuckle, she closed the door. When she turned around, Zoltar was standing there with his cup of coffee. "Ready to have that talk?"

She crossed her arms over her chest. "What talk? The one where I claimed you as a mate in a room full of royals?"

With a smirk, he took a sip of his coffee in a failed attempt at being nonchalant. "Yeah, that."

His pants hung low on his hips and the white T-shirt that clung to his arms and chest only accented his deep tan. She fought not to get sexually distracted from a very real conversation that needed to happen.

She stared at him for a second longer. "Let's take our coffee outside. It looks like a beautiful morning." Walking past him, she scurried to the table to reclaim her cup. After a quick duck into the kitchen to refill it, she met him at the patio door. Once outside they took a seat at a small table and chairs just outside her door.

Closing her eyes she tilted her face toward the sun, feeling the warmth lick her skin, before she turned her head to face him. "You've made your feelings clear. I've been the one holding back out of old concerns. It became clear to me, I was being foolish. In all my years I never felt so alive. Never, have I felt so drawn to someone and I'm positive it has nothing to do with hormones."

He kept his expression blank as he studied her words. She felt as if he understood her, so she continued. "During the fight yesterday, you didn't hesitate to let me battle alongside you. You allowed me to defend our home as your equal, not some weak female who needed guarding.

That showed me respect. The fact you took my flank to defend while I had the scumbag, well, showed you cared. For all of the bad reputations Centaurs have acquired over centuries, you've undone every single myth." She took a sip of her coffee to give pause. "Well?"

Running his fingers through his blond locks, he looked at her, brows pulled together forming a crease in the middle. "I, uh…I need the Lycanthropy professor to answer some questions for me, if it's okay."

It wasn't the response she'd expected. She blinked a few times and shook her head. "I'm sorry?"

With a slight tilt of his head he leaned in a little closer. "I have a few questions about Lycans I'd like answered, about mates and bonding. Would you mind answering those for me, since you are the Lycanthropy professor? I can't think of anyone more qualified."

"Oh! Oh, sure. I didn't think…" *Of course he has questions, you dimwit. He doesn't know much about his Lycan half, nor what it is to be you.* "Sure. What questions do you have?"

Leaning back in his chair, he crossed his feet at the ankles, elbows on the arm rests with his fingers folded and took a deep breath. "Lycans can be married or mated, but not bonded. Yes?"

Oh. He's worried about the bonding. Does he want a bond? "Yes. I suppose. It would be extremely rare though. Lycan lovers are, uh, well, we have a predisposition to bond. Our wolves sort of take over for that part, not fully, mind you. We stay in human form and as you saw, the teeth protrude, sometimes the snout comes out a bit."

Expressionless, he bobbed his head. "And what happens when there is a bond?"

Now it was Wendy who leaned in on her elbows. "It's hard to explain as someone who has yet to bond herself. I think our bonding will be a bit different. Grace actually warned me of as much. Normally, however, there's a small bite and a lick of blood. The couple is then tied to each other's thoughts and feelings. A bond is a forever thing.

There's no going back once it happens. Other shifter species have similar bonds. Though I have to admit, I don't know anything about interspecies bonding."

Her heart beat a little faster as she answered his questions. Was he weighing his options or just making sure he knew what would happen? She could feel her shirt beginning to cling to her as the nervous sweat took hold.

"What sort of warning did Grace give you?" He sipped at his coffee gazing at her.

"When she and Roman bonded, they received the memories of their ancestors. Such a thing doesn't occur in a normal Lycan bond. Because you are the king, there is a chance; one or both of us will have the same experience. I will lose contact with my wolf for a while as she makes a transformation." She took a deep breath. "Any more questions?"

Sitting up straight in his chair he placed his coffee cup on the table. "As the Centaur Queen you will have to think of my people as your people as well. Can a full-blooded Lycan beauty such as yourself see that as a possibility? Are you willing to accept our customs? They might be vastly different than yours."

She hadn't thought about that aspect of a mating with Zoltar. The weight of it caused her shoulders to fall forward as her only real consideration had been on the two of them.

"Honestly, I haven't thought that far ahead. However, we Lycans move fast when it comes to our mates. We always have. And I can tell you this much, I'm already thinking of the staff as my pack. It's no small feat and it did happen quickly, even when I didn't think it was a possibility. We don't have to move any further in this relationship until we're both ready. For now, I am comfortable claiming you as mine—and I am yours. When we want to move forward, we can, and will."

"One more question."

She noticed the grin spreading across his face. "Yes?"

"Do you want children?"

She put her hand on her chest as if to keep it firmly in place. She tried to stop the tears forming in her eyes by taking a deep breath in through her nose. "Very much."

"That makes me very happy. I have to say, Wendy...I seem to have known from the moment I laid eyes on you. It was as if an alarm went off in my head. I *had* to know you. Something inside me insisted on it, and it wasn't the wolf. It was an instinct I've never experienced before. You must understand, however, my kind hasn't experienced marriage or mating. None of us still alive today, anyway. I will more than likely make horrid mistakes. When I do, you'll need to tell me."

She burst into laughter. "Uh no. I won't. When we bond, you'll know when I'm pissed. You'll feel it."

His eyes widened. "Good to know."

She wiped her eyes to rid herself of the remainder of lingering moisture. "As I understand it, it's best for us to let the bond happen naturally and try not to plan it out. It's sort of a call of nature, if you will. But we can restrain ourselves if it tries to happen and we're not ready."

He shook his head. "I don't feel a need to wait. Do you?"

Biting her lip she considered the situation. "Yes. I need to spend time with your men. I need to know them in order to affirmatively say I can consider them my pack. I can't really say beforehand in a true heartfelt manner."

"One tiny thing," he scooted off of his chair and knelt down in front of her, "just a small detail."

"Okay?"

"We are a herd, not a pack. So, try to use *that* word with them. It'll show a sign of respect they'll appreciate." He grabbed her hand. "And they'll love you as much as I do."

Emotions boiled over. She leaned in, planting her lips firmly against his—elated, she'd finally found her mate. She found him in an unlikely place. Colin's words echoed through her mind. *"Perhaps, we are holding you back."* At the time, the words wounded but...he had been right. Her mate was out in the world and they had to find each other.

"Combat training starts in thirty minutes," he said when she released him. "Wear something comfortable." He winked as he pushed off the ground and stood to his feet. Holding out his hand for her, he lifted her to her feet. "Thank you for the breakfast. It was wonderful."

* * * *

"Archery has been a staple among Centaurs since the beginning. Humans have their guns. They're powerful and effective. A bow and arrow, when wielded by a skilled master, is nearly silent. With the right blades, it can kill on contact. Now, Centaurs are also known for their adaptability." Theron reached up and grabbed a branch off a tree, breaking it.

The Fae gasped at the damage to the tree.

"Now I have a strong club to use. Its length keeps my attackers at a distance."

"And..." Zoltar stepped to the front of the class, slapping his Beta in the back. "Even a nut can be a weapon. Allow me to demonstrate." He picked up a slingshot and an acorn. He aimed at a gallon jug, pulled back and released the nut. It pierced a hole through the jug. "It's about velocity and the surface of the projectile. Again, it's very quiet, making it effective in a sneak attack."

Wendy studied each movement carefully, taking mental notes of each instruction. They broke up into groups to learn archery and how to use the sling shot. The bows the Centaurs used were the largest she'd ever seen, intricately carved and ornate. The arrows contained sharp blades, designed for maximum devastation. Normal sized bows were handed out to the class. Turned out, she wasn't half bad at archery.

"You're a natural," Zoltar whispered in her ear.

Heat permeated every cell in her body. "You're distracting me, Professor."

"Artemis!" He bellowed. Another Centaur trotted over, and then shifted to human form. "Please work with Ms. Baker on her aim. Her form is near perfect. Show her line of sight." He winked at her and turned his attention to another student.

Artemis tilted her elbow up. "Perfect. I'm very impressed. You don't really need help, just practice."

She shot four more arrows, hitting the target center the last two times.

"Now," Zoltar announced, "stay in your groups. We're about to learn combat techniques."

She placed the bow on the rack near her and turned her attention back to Artemis.

"Let's start with the Gnomes," he said.

A little male Gnome walked up next to Artemis, his dark curly hair tucked in a knit cap.

"Tell me, how do you fight?" He took a knee as he waited for the answer.

The little man shrugged. "We don't. We hide or run."

The Centaur gave one firm nod. "Let's look at your strengths. Your people are good climbers. Yes?"

The little man bobbed his head. "Oh yes. We're swift climbers."

An evil grin spread across the Centaur's face. "That's perfect." He turned to everyone else as he stood. "Now, we've established they're fantastic climbers. They're small and agile. So, the best option is to scale your assailant and attack—eyes, nose, and mouth. The faster you move, the more confused your opponent will be. On three, I'm sorry, what's your name?"

"Bart."

"On three, Bart. Climb up to my face as fast as you can."

Her heart raced. What if the little guy slipped? What would keep him from being thrown to his death?

"Three!" Artemis yelled.

Bart was a blur as he scaled the Centaur.

She had no idea they were *that* swift, making her feel foolish for lifting Mary constantly.

Whoop, whoosh, whoop, whoosh. The sound caused her to jump just in time to see an arrow narrowly miss her hear.

"Sorry!" Following the sound of the voice, she saw a female Dwarf whose face had turned pale.

The Centaur instructor jerked the bow out of her hand. "That was reckless!"

With a deep breath, she tried to shake it off and pay attention to Artemis's instructions. *Could that have been on purpose?*

"Now, from behind me, you can do several things. If you have a knife and it's you or your attacker, stab here in the neck or throat. If you don't have a sharp object, then use your hands. Pull on their nose, gouge their eyes. Do as much damage as you can. If they can't see you, they can't find you to hurt you. You may be tiny, but you don't have to be a victim. Use it to your advantage. Let their assumption that you're frail be their downfall."

They practiced the maneuver a few times. Each time she was equally frightened and impressed by Bart.

"Excuse me," she interrupted.

"Yes?" The Centaur instructor scowled at her.

"I have two questions, if I may. First, what if they're thrown? I mean, an adult male could easily throw them a good distance."

Artemis smiled over his shoulder at Bart. "Wanna show her?"

"Sure." He shrugged.

He reached over his shoulder, snatched the little man by the collar and tossed him like a football.

Certain she was watching the murder of a Gnome, a scream ripped through her throat. But to her surprise, Bart twisted in mid-flight like a cat and landed on his hands and feet. As he walked back toward the group, her mouth dropped.

"Gnomes are built a lot like cats and squirrels. They're very springy. They can fall from tall heights without injury." The instructor assured. "They're a very impressive species."

The group applauded Bart as he made it back to them.

"You had another question?" Artemis asked as he ran his hand over his blond locks and licked his lips.

"How would a group of Gnomes defend against, say, a herd of Centaur?"

Zoltar hadn't steered her wrong. The instructor gave a slight bow of the head, a sign of respect. "In all honesty, they're best bet would be to wound enough to make an escape. It isn't that a Gnome could not kill a Centaur. But there would be a lot of unnecessary collateral damage. They might be fierce but if any herd or pack comes after them, they will lose a lot of their people."

She nodded and fought the urge to celebrate her tiny victory. "Thank you."

"Excellent questions. Your turn." He motioned to the area next to him.

She took a deep cleansing breath before walking up next to him. "Much of our fighting will take place in human form so if we're spotted, we're not spotted in true form. The humans just can't handle that sort of reality. So, Wendy, as a Lycan you're large, swift and powerful. But as a human woman, what are you going to do if I attack you?"

"I'm sorry, but I don't have a good answer except that I would fight back." Heat radiated around her neck, worried she'd appeared foolish.

"Good, now, let's look at how." He stepped closer, directly in front of her. "Let's focus on disabling your attacker, just like with Bart."

She shook her hands and readied herself for attack.

"Vulnerabilities are eyes, nose, throat, and stomach, right? Without vision, I can't see you to attack. The nose, well, it can blind as well, I'll get to that in a minute. A strike in the throat will cause the assailant to gasp for air. A strike in the right area of the neck can cause a heart arrhythmia. The groin is obvious." He pointed to the butt of his hand above his wrist. "This part of your hand can hurt worse than a fist." He made a slow motion toward her face, pressing the butt of his hand to the bottom of her nose. "Moving quickly to hit like this will bust someone's nose. When the nose breaks…vision goes white for a split second, giving you time to get a few more hits in. That's when I'd go for the throat. Now they can't see or breathe. This will allow for ample time to kill, or flee, whatever is necessary."

He continued the instructions until they sparred on a mat. She clocked him a few good times and kicked him a little too hard in the leg. It buckled under him.

"Oh Goddess! I'm so sorry." She tried to assist him back to his feet.

"Sorry? That was perfect!" He laughed and slapped his knee. "You have a warrior's heart."

Looking around, she found Zoltar applauding her from the other side of the practice area.

"Okay," he stood up and shook his leg. "Let's give the Pixie a try, shall we?"

She rejoined the group as the Pixie was afforded her turn practicing. Watching as her classmates all sparred with their new skills; she felt a sense of relief. They could defend themselves well. With training, they'd be unstoppable. Perhaps she didn't have to worry so much.

Class was dismissed for lunch, though all she truly wanted was a shower.

"Impressive." She heard Zoltar's voice behind her.

"Oh well, thank you. Artemis is a good teacher." She looped her arm in his.

"Learn anything useful?"

"Well, on a non-combat level, I now know I don't have to squat down for Mary to climb on and off my back.

Who knew they could climb like that?" She pulled her shoulders up and let them fall, feeling foolish.

He shrugged. "I did."

"What? And you didn't say anything? You watched me squat down knowing I didn't have to?" She slugged him in the bicep.

He chuckled. "You were being sweet. How was I supposed to put a stop to that?"

She rolled her eyes as they walked in to the building. "Thanks."

Stretching one arm over her shoulders he pulled her in with a squeeze. "Herd is going for a run this afternoon. Care to join us?"

It would be the perfect opportunity to bond with them, to see what they were like while separated from the others. She smiled up at him. "I'd be delighted."

Over lunch they chatted about the lessons, about the prisoner in the basement, and reveled in the fact that the soot had been cleaned and the building didn't look any worse for the wear.

"Might I join you?" Grace asked. Roman stood behind her, his smile wide.

"Of course, sit!" She tossed her hand at the area beside her. As if they'd have to ask.

"So, you know when you have a wild idea, or your thoughts are strong, I intercept them whether or not I'm trying," Grace started as she picked up her sandwich.

"That's most unfortunate." The heat rose around her face. She felt her cheeks burn hot.

"You'll learn to put up a wall eventually. The point is I called Nala about making room for some Gnomes. She's delighted and already has Xander meeting with Mary to go over building needs." She moved her gaze toward Zoltar. "I would like to ask one more favor of you, my friend."

He wiped his hands on a napkin and tossed it on the table. "Anything."

With a grin and a nod, she continued. "Would you be

so kind as to get the list of needs from Xander and draw up two or three blueprints we could use for their homes?"

He put up his hands. "It would be an honor. I've already been thinking about a way to make them miniature sized tools so they're not so dependent upon others. They really do want to contribute the work from what I gathered from Mary."

Roman leaned ahead to look past Grace at Wendy. "You're amazing. You've been given full credit for this idea. Nala is excited to lead a pack into the new world and this is a huge step toward building a real sense of community with the supernaturals. Colin is contacting packs across the country to see if they're interested as well."

She'd done it. A small suggestion, an idea really, and the lives of an entire species could be improved exponentially. She'd doubted herself when they asked her to be Headmistress. She didn't really think she had the skillset required. But now? She'd managed to figure out transportation for the Gnomes, and a new living arrangement. These had been her ideas—hers.

What else could she do?

TEN

"Wendy, this will be your office!" Grace opened the door.

She dropped her bag on the floor. "You've got to be kidding me!" A large mahogany desk and black leather chair sat in the center of an enormous room, lined with light oak bookshelves. A private bathroom sat to the right of the room and to the left was a closet to store her things. Three large area rugs covered the stone floor, warming the environment further. "It's so beautiful."

"I'm glad you like it. The desktop computer is connected to your laptop and cellphone. All the files will sync up, Xander's bright idea, of course. He wanted things to be as easy for you as possible. He will be here in a few minutes to walk you through the student files." Grace put her arm around her shoulder and gave her a squeeze. "Make yourself at home."

* * * *

The month had flown by. Students had arrived early to get settled and obtain their schedules. Xander had made her job extremely easy, though with such a large student body, it was time consuming. Tiffany had volunteered to be her assistant until everything was finished.

She managed to ferret out a bit of time for Mary, and a bit more than that for Zoltar. He didn't complain when she was so exhausted she'd fall asleep before they could be intimate. More than that, he'd brought lunch to her office so they could dine together. They ran at night with the herd, and most of the time, the Gnomes would hitch rides on her or one of the Centaurs.

Bonding with the herd wasn't as much of a challenge as she suspected. Most respected her as Zoltar's mate and welcomed her with open arms. Theron had worked with her on her archery and combat skills in both human and wolf form.

A side benefit was the excellent physical condition she was in. She felt spry as a pup, her arms and legs feeling stronger than ever before.

School would start once the weekend had passed. A team had been assembled to track down the Separatists and as long as they were on the run, they didn't seem to bother with the school. The staff had relaxed, though patrols remained steady.

She sat at her desk, studying her files. She hoped she'd placed the students in the right classes, but was prepared to make changes should the need arise.

"What are you doing working so late?" It was Barb, Grace's friend. Her blonde hair was pulled in a tight ponytail at the top of her head and it swayed as she walked into Wendy's office.

She studied her for a moment. The woman had been noticeably scarce and now she was barging in her office. Still, she forced a smile. "Making sure I'm prepared for the first day. You know, dotting the I's and whatnot. What about you? Big plans for this evening?"

Barb leaned back in the chair, putting her boots on her beautiful desk. "Well, there is a pub in town. It's owned by a Werepanther. I considered getting a drink with Grace, but she's busy as usual." Rolling her eyes, she released an obnoxious sigh.

"Well, she is the Lycan Queen and has a lot on her plate. I'm sure you understand." Something about this woman had bothered Wendy when they met. Something still bothered her.

"I suppose. I just miss the Grace I had in college."

With a huff, she tilted her head. "You mean, when she thought she was a human, lost in a world that didn't have a place for her?"

A pout protruded from her bottom lip. "When you put it that way…"

She wanted to get away from this woman before she said something truly offensive. She stood, throwing her bag over her shoulder. "The staff here is quite large. You should get to know the others. I haven't really seen you around much, maybe if you put yourself out there."

Barb's left eyebrow shot up. She'd gotten the hint of being dismissed and it obviously displeased her. "Well, I had some things to get caught up on. Then there was the Pixie who died and the bombing. I just stayed in my room where it was safe."

What the hell kind of Werepanther hides? She fought not to react.

"This one smells wrong." Her wolf stirred.

"I understand. Now, if you'll excuse me." She walked to her door and stood next to the opening, urging her guest to leave.

"Sitting around isn't really the way I wanted to spend a Friday night." Barb huffed as she stormed out of her office.

After a deep, cleansing breath, she locked the door and headed off toward the West wing and down the stairs to her living quarters. Dinner had already passed but she'd planned to have drinks and conversation with Zoltar by the fire. She really wanted to spend time with him since time had been a commodity which she truly lacked over the past month.

The halls were buzzing with students, eager to start their new adventure. The Pixies had a gathering planned for them not just to entertain them, but to keep them from getting into trouble. The noise had increased as she passed the dining hall. Music echoed through the hall along with laughter. The combination of the two had Wendy smiling when she rounded the corner to her hall.

"That's a beautiful smile."

"Z! I was just thinking about you." She opened her arms and ran into him, kissing his cheek and he lifted her up. "I'm finally free to spend some quality time with you, if you'll have me."

"Ha, ha! I have plans for you tonight. We're dining on the roof." He held up his hands, "I know, I know, you had a sandwich at four. Let's put your things in your apartment and go on up."

A sandwich wasn't really fitting for a Lycan meal. Combine that with the elation of spending quality time with him and she was damned near giddy. She skipped forward to her door, unlocked it, set her things inside and locked it behind her. "Ready!"

With another husky laugh, he scooped her hand in his. He led her to a winding staircase at the back end of a hall to a door. When he opened it, she saw the entire Centaur herd gathered.

"Sagittarius is above us tonight, the archer. We like to have a small celebration in recognition." Zoltar spoke in her ear, his hot breath on her cheek. "It's a very Centaur thing to do."

"Show me," she looked at the stars, eager to learn.

He pointed at a group of twinkling lights that didn't look much like anything to her. Still she smiled and nodded. When her gaze came back to the crowd, she realized they'd all watched to see her reaction. Her heart felt like it missed a beat or two.

"Can someone tell me something about Sagittarius? I'm afraid I know next to nothing about him." She swallowed, and looked up at Zoltar.

"Bring her over here, Z. Don't leave her standing there!" Theron tossed a wadded napkin at him.

The others laughed.

"I'm sorry, but our fearless leader seems to be a bit befuddled." Continuing the teasing, Theron looped his arm around hers and dragged her to the long table they had set up.

"Red or white?" A young Centaur she recognized held up a bottle of each.

She smiled at him, thankful they all seemed delighted with her company. "Red, please."

He filled her glass before reclaiming his seat. She looked around the table, their faces eager.

Zoltar's warm palm rested on her thigh as he claimed a seat next to her. "Sagittarius represents the Centaur Chiron, which is why we hold him dear in our hearts, he's our ancestor. He was more than an archer. A gentle being, he was also musician, physician, and tutor to Achilles, Jason, and Hercules. His arrow is pointing at Antares, the bright red heart of Scorpius." A young Centaur handed him a tabletop telescope. He placed it on the table and looked through the glass. "Here, that star. He's pointing it at Scorpius to avenge Orion, who was slain by the scorpion's sting."

After looking through the telescope, she took a sip of her wine, and then placed her glass on the table as she carefully considered her words. "I can see why he's celebrated then. A pack, or in your case, a herd, should always defend and avenge their own. Anything less would be nothing more than cowardly." They avenged their own. *Is this a warning?*

"Wendy," Theron stood as he spoke. She turned her attention toward him. "We're all aware of your connection to our king. As you know, we haven't had a queen for a very long time. We brought you here, on the celebration of Sagittarius, to tell you that should you choose to take on the title and responsibility as our first queen; we would all die to protect you. We would serve you well; treat you with honor, kindness, and respect. Respect not only as our queen, but as the fierce warrior you've shown yourself to be."

Words evading her, she glanced around at the stripling faces, eager to have her as their queen. Ready to accept her for who and what she is—and could be. They needn't go through the pomp and circumstance. She'd already made up her mind. She loved Zoltar and began loving his herd, those she knew anyway.

This hadn't been the quaint sipping of drinks by the fire she'd planned, but it certainly had an effect. Her heart swelled and soared to new heights. Yet the words weren't coming.

"It will be my honor," she muttered, knowing in her heart her words weren't enough. She raised her glass. "To new beginnings."

With reverent silence, they all lifted their glasses.

"You've chosen wisely," Theron nod toward Zoltar.

She let out a quiet laugh. "Let's just hope I serve you as well as you serve me."

A deep voice came from her left. "If I may?"

She turned to face him. She recognized him from combat training. His name was Prometheus and he was usually very quiet, but commanding. "Of course."

"Ma'am, I think you may be missing it. The reason we all brought you here, on this night. It's not simply to swear an oath to you, or to share a celebration. You may be missing the correlation between you and our ancestor Chiron." He smiled though it seemed to be more directed at Zoltar as his gaze shifted behind her. "See, Chiron was an archer, he was a great warrior. Our kind back then, well, we were...shall we say, a bit rowdy. He chose a nobler path. He was kind and gentle. He was a teacher—a

Centaur who took time to teach legends. You, ma'am, you're a fierce warrior when it's required, defending our home, our people. When it's not, you care for others. You put the needs of the Gnomes front and center and worked with our king and other leaders to improve their lives. You are gentle, it is your nature. It matters not whether you're Centaur or Lycan, you were made in Chiron's image. It's clear to us all."

Her hands shook as a tear stung her eye. To have someone, an entire group, see her as such a person was overwhelming. "Thank you," she squeaked as she smoothed her hands on her pants.

"I think we've given her enough for one night." Zoltar moved his and over hers. "Let us celebrate."

Once the others took their attention off of her she turned to him. "That was overwhelming to say the least."

Half a smile spread across the left side of his face. "You wouldn't have believed it unless you heard it from them. They've been after me to do this for two weeks. Have you any idea the difficulty trying to calm an anxious herd of Centaur?" He laughed. "It's damned near impossible."

She squeezed his hand. "I've been worried I've neglected you. I've been so exhausted and—"

"Exactly. You've only been getting around four hours of sleep a night. I had feared you took on too much responsibility, but Grace assured me, once the class schedules were handled, you'd have more time to rest."

She shook her head as she laughed. "It didn't help that I double and triple checked everything, worried I would miss something important."

"That would be sleep." He leaning in. "And tonight I mean to insure you get an adequate amount of it. No waking early and making breakfast. You'll sleep in and I will take care of you." He forced his brows together and playfully wagged his finger in her face. "I insist."

She scooped up her wine and leaned back in her chair.

"You will get no argument from me!"

In her peripheral, she saw Theron wave his hand. Almost instantly, the staff placed plates in front of them containing steak, rice, and green beans. Wendy's mouth watered.

Conversation was light during the meal. When the plates were cleared, liquor was served. The Centaurs were served Ouzo and a Lycan whiskey was placed in front of her.

"What's this?" She held the glass in his face.

"I'm sorry? It's Lycan whiskey. I thought you liked it."

"Well, when in Rome." She snatched his glass from him and tossed it back. The warm licorice liquid warmed her throat as it slid down, giving her a tiny shiver at the end. "That's nice."

Grinning he took her glass of whiskey and drank it for her. "I wish we could get absinthe, but it's getting more and more difficult to find."

"Oh, well," she wagged her hand in the air, "you should talk to Gustav. He always has absinthe at his parties. I'm sure he'd help you."

"Did I hear my name?" Gustav appeared behind her.

It had the expected effect. The Centaurs all jumped to their feet, startled by the sudden appearance of him.

"Relax, he is a friend." She laughed and stood from her chair to offer her hand.

He gave it a cold gentle kiss. "To what do I owe the pleasure?"

"Gustav, have you met Zoltar?"

The vamp smiled at the Centaur King. "Of course."

"Wait? Did I summon you by mistake?" She searched her mind. She had only mentioned his name, not called out to him.

"Oh my dear, part of the witch's protective spell alerts me when my name is mentioned. I wanted to ensure I could defend this building and my friends." He turned to Zoltar. "It is nice to see you again."

He nodded, relaxing his shoulders and motioning for his men to stand down. "Likewise."

She looped her arm in his. "Z was just telling me, they're drinking Ouzo because they are having a difficult time finding absinthe. I remembered you always have it at your parties. Perhaps you could introduce him to your supplier."

"Well that's fairly simple, I am the manufacturer." His fangy grin showed a hint of pride that made her smile. "I would be happy to work out an arrangement. However, for tonight, it's my treat. I'll be back in a moment."

When he vanished the Centaurs jumped once more.

She turned to them. "Listen, Vampires do that. Gustav is a friend. You'll have to learn to relax a bit. I know it can be disconcerting, someone appearing out of thin air next to you, but really, you can trust him. He has been a great ally to the Belfast pack for years. Much of his money went to build this school."

He appeared again with an entire case of absinthe.

"Whoa! Goddess! That's a lot." Theron leaned over the table to get a better view.

With a smile and a nod, Gustav said, "It is my understanding Centaurs can hold a fair amount of liquor. I didn't want you to run out."

She leaned into Zoltar and whispered. "Would you invite him to stay?"

He nodded. "Would you care to join us?"

Wendy swore she could feel the air whip around her with the collective gasp of the herd.

"Oh that would be marvelous! They should really get to know you!" She touched his arm. "Please stay and have a drink."

"Have you ever known me to turn down hospitality?" He handed the case of liquor to a Centaur standing nearest him, pulling a bottle out. He placed it on the table and smiled at Wendy. "One more trip." This time, when he reappeared he had a box containing spoons and sugar cubes, sitting on top of a case containing special glasses that had a small bulbous area toward the bottom. "One cannot toss back absinthe like any other spirit."

He asked for pitchers of ice water then demonstrated the complicated but proper procedure for preparing each glass. He placed a slotted utensil on top of the glass, then a sugar cube on top. He drizzled water on the cube dissolving it into the liquor below. He handed the first glass to Wendy.

The strong anise flavor hit her at once. Then, as it rolled over her tongue she tasted distinctive flowery notes. "Wow!"

"Wow, indeed." Gustav watched the others as they prepared their drinks, giving instructions to those floundering.

"I thought you set it on fire?" Theron asked.

"Blasphemy!" Gustav bellowed with a laugh. "One does not cook good quality absinthe." He grunted something that sounded like, "Bohemians."

She watched the vampire interact with the herd. Their apprehension had subsided and they began their usual banter, teasing. She hadn't recalled a time when he looked happier. She wondered if he was lonely.

"All of the time, my dear." His voice was in her head. She'd heard he had the ability but had never experienced it for herself. *"Thank you for inviting me to stay. I'm having a wonderful time and I seem to be making friends. Do you think they're less frightened of me?"*

She smiled at him, slightly embarrassed that he was listening to her thoughts, but pleased he was in good company.

When you appear and disappear it is a bit startling. Now that you are acquainted, I think they like you. The fact that you're getting them piss-faced drunk isn't hurting.

"Perhaps you could mention, at some point, that they don't smell appetizing to me at all?"

Spitting her drink, she snatched a napkin off of the

table to cover her mouth as she laughed. She dabbed at her mouth and then her pants which now had absinthe sprayed all over them.

"You okay?" Zoltar laughed with her.

She wagged her hand. "Yes, yes, I'm fine. A little tipsy, maybe."

"Come on," he said as he stood, "let's get you to bed."

"Goodnight everyone. Thank you for a wonderful evening." She looked at Gustav. "Until next time."

"Please, let me save you the stairs. Absinthe can really affect depth perception." He walked over to her. "Just picture your hallway. I can have you both outside your door in a second."

Zoltar looked at her with wide eyes.

"It's painless. I've done it before," she assured him. She looped her arm in his and took Gustav's hand. She closed her eyes and envisioned the markings of her hall. Instantly, they were there.

"That was wild!" Zoltar blinked rapidly.

The vampire gave a soft chuckle. "Wild. Yes. It used to be quite fun. Thank you two for a wonderful evening. It has been a pleasure."

"Thank you! You made it a party." She threw her arms around him. He stiffened briefly before relaxing in an embrace.

"I do not recall the last hug I received." He sniffed.

She released him in time to see a bloody tear escape his eye. "That's horrible. Hugs are nice. No more kissy hand." *Kissy hand? Yep. I'm drunk.*

He must have heard her thoughts because he snickered.

"You'll get a hug from now on," she said with a firm nod. "No excuse for any creature not to feel a warm embrace."

He turned to Zoltar who shocked the vamp with an enormous hug of his own. When he released him, he slapped him on the shoulder. "What? No bloody tears for me?"

The vamp laughed, shook his head and disappeared.

"Okay, that's one skill I covet," he admitted.

With a nod, she pushed open her door. "I feel like I could sleep for a week."

Her apartment looked odd. The walls were wavy as was the floor. "Did something happen? Did we get bombed again?"

His husky laugh startled her. "What?"

"Look at the walls!" Her finger appeared wavy to her as she pointed at the crooked walls.

"Absinthe sort of does that. It's okay. I promise everything is as it should be." He bent down and scooped her up. "But I'll get you in bed safely."

Tucking her head between his neck and shoulder, she relented. "Okay." She'd had plans for a *few* drinks and a lot of lovemaking. Instead, she had a lot of drinks and her vision was wonky.

"Tonight, I take care of you," he whispered as he placed her on the bed.

Looking up at him, even the ceiling above him swirled and curved. She wasn't sure how she'd make love to him without getting dizzy.

He pulled her shirt over her head and tossed it on the dresser. Placing his hands on the top of her shoulders, he pushed her, yet held on to her, easing her down on the bed. After pulling her shoes and pants off, he stood, smiling down at her. "Roll over, please."

With less grace that was suitable for a Lycan, she rolled until she was on her stomach. She felt the bed dip as he straddled her hips. His warm hands began kneading her shoulders.

"That feels like heaven." She moaned as he continued working her sore muscles.

"Good, now just relax." His voice was low and soft, as if he was afraid to wake someone. His hands moved to her lower back and hips, caressing and massaging.

She'd never had a massage before. It was the most

heavenly feeling she had experienced outside of making love to him. Darkness fell on her as she slipped into a dream state.

ELEVEN

The aroma of coffee permeated the air. Wendy had to force her eyes to open. Her head felt heavy, fighting against her lifting it off the pillow. "Oh, my head." There was a slight throbbing behind her eyes. She considered closing them again and resting her enormous head on the pillow. Absinthe.

She cursed the green spirit as she swung her feet to the floor. Looking down she noticed she was still sporting her bra and panties from the day before. After shuffling to the closet and tossing the undergarments in her hamper, she pulled on her robe and tied it closed. After a painful shuffle to the bathroom she made her way to the kitchen where Zoltar stood with a cup of coffee and some buttery toast.

"Oh you're a godsend."

"You can have this," he said holding up the cup of coffee, "after you drink this." In his other hand was a glass of ice water. "You need to rehydrate."

If all that stood between her and a cup of coffee was a glass of water, she'd gladly cool her hot pipes. She took the water and swigged it down. "May I have my coffee now?"

He smiled, handing it over. "I said I'd take care of you. I didn't say you'd like it." He shrugged. "With your Lycan genes you should feel pretty good once your body absorbs the water."

"Thank you. Sorry, I'm a bit out of it. Aren't you having breakfast?" She looked at the solitary plate of toast.

"I finished lunch a few hours ago."

Spinning on her heel, she turned to face the clock. "Three! I've slept my whole day away!"

"You needed it. Let's have a seat." He kissed her forehead before walking out of the kitchen. She followed him to the living room.

"I can't believe I lost a whole day," she said with a pout.

He tilted his head, his lips curving into a soft smile. "Eat your toast," he said, nudging her plate.

Picking up the toast, she furrowed her brow and took a bite. It felt like dry sawdust as it scraped against her dry mouth. She choked it down and chased it with coffee. "I can't believe I'm hung over. I'm sorry you had to see me like that, last night, I mean."

"You were overly exhausted and absinthe is fairly strong." He stroked her thigh. "Honestly, you were fine until your vision went a little wonky. Even then, it isn't like you made a scene."

She thanked her Lycan genes noting that her headache was already subsiding. She upended her coffee, drinking every drop before returning to the kitchen for more water. "That was wonderful last night, by the way. The massage lulled me right to sleep." She called out from the kitchen while she poured another cup of coffee. She made her way back, sitting to face him.

"You're welcome."

She gazed at him, this man who'd taken care of her, who'd swept her off her feet. Her heart couldn't grow for this beautiful creature any more or it may burst. "And the dinner, the party, was wonderful."

He nodded, seemingly pleased to hear it.

"My intentions for last night, however, were to have a few glasses of wine by the fire. To tell you I was ready to move forward with our relationship—and that was before the herd's declaration. It didn't change my mind, but it certainly solidified my decision." Leaning forward, she laced her fingers in his. Her gaze traveled from their intertwined fingers up to his eyes. Her mouth fell open when she noticed a tear, glistening in his eye.

"I cannot tell you how happy I am." He cleared his throat. "I promise to take the best care of you, Wendy. I swear it."

Fighting back tears of her own, she leaned in and kissed him on the cheek. "I believe you."

"I'll draw you a bath." He stood from the couch. "By the time you're ready, we can go to the hall and join the others for dinner. Your stomach should be ready for a proper meal by then. Tonight, we'll relax with a less aggressive beverage by the fire. How does that sound?"

Draw me a bath? Is he for real? No one has drawn me a bath since I was a child.

* * * *

The noise from the dining hall was much louder when filled with the student body. They took a seat at the staff table next to Roman and Grace. On the other side of Roman sat a sour-faced Barb. Wendy couldn't imagine what reason she had to be so grumpy.

Conversation was light and cheerful, despite the grump, as excitement for the new school term had built.

"Do you know what you're going to say at the Pre-Term assembly?" Zoltar addressed Grace as he crammed a chunk of beef in his mouth.

She shrugged. "I'll keep it short and sweet, introduce the staff and wish them all a successful school year. It shouldn't be that difficult."

Gustav appeared behind Grace and Roman, leaned forward whispering something to them. Grace dropped her fork. Roman placed a protective hand on her back as he nodded to the vampire.

She scooted from the table and slowly walked to the head of the room. "Can I have your attention please?" Her voice boomed.

Wendy's heart gave a start. She'd never heard Grace speak so loudly—didn't even know it was possible. She wondered if it wasn't a royal talent.

When the room quieted she gave a nod and put her hands together. "I want to welcome the students and thank you for arriving early to schedule classes. I'm sure it hasn't been the most exciting few weeks for you, though I am pleased to see most of you used the time to explore and familiarize yourself with the campus. We'll have a brief assembly Monday at seven thirty. There is a staff meeting in five minutes. Thank you."

She hurried back to the table. The staff all rose and filed out of the hall, following her to the conference room. Zoltar grabbed Wendy's hand, offering a gentle squeeze of comfort as they made their way. Once everyone was inside, she closed the door behind her.

Her gaze fell on the floor as she approached the table and took a seat. "There has been a development. The Separatists released a video online showing themselves shift. It's gone viral." She looked at Xander, "Kill the Internet and cable and put up the net."

He pulled a tablet computer out of his bag and tapped the screen a few times. "Done."

"We anticipated this situation, or something similar. Xander has a net up. It's an invisible net, that can kill all cellular signals from getting through the property so kids with smartphones can't access the news. The group that has been hunting the Separatists is doing damage control now. We'll turn it back on when we can spin it. As of right now, we don't know how much danger we are in."

Worried looks flew around the room. True fear. Humans hunted animals and to them, they couldn't be anything but. They couldn't come out of hiding. Not until they were organized, with their own system of government established.

"We should consider not doing any spin control," Zoltar blurted, shocking Wendy with the same thought process. "Instead, let us organize. Let us establish our government and send a delegation into the authorities to attempt coming out as a peaceful and civilized society. Show the humans they don't have to fear us."

"Humans fear everything that is different than them," Ella objected. "They fear other humans who are different. How do you think they'll accept us?"

Roman cleared his throat. "Ms. Rutger? Any opinions?"

All eyes shifted to one of the few humans in the room. She stood, her face solemn. "Ella is right. Humans do terrible things to one another. But you should prepare yourselves. Even if you make the video out to be a fake, there will be a lot of people who still believe in it. They'll look for shifters, Pixies and Fae. You can't hide forever. Not in this day in age. There's too much technology and not enough places to hide. My advice would be to do your spin control and prepare for the worst. Get your government organized immediately. Even if it's sloppy. Use the American system here. It'll make them feel more at ease. Get word to the other countries to do the same, if they wish and follow the leadership structure of everything but a dictatorship. Most find that to be the most brutal and the least diplomatic." She put her hand on her neck. "And I do not mean any offense to anyone here, but my understanding is that you are only now, after centuries, integrating and becoming a society of one. You're very much behind the rest of civilization. Your kind didn't go through the Civil War, Suffrage, and Affirmative Action...none of the human rights that have given them their moral code of today. You can't expect others to accept you if you don't accept each other."

Shuffling sounds next to her caused Wendy to seek out the noise. She spotted Barb fidgeting in her chair like she was about to piss her pants. Scowling at the woman, she looked back to Grace who also took note of Barb's odd behavior.

Beauregard shot out of his chair, stormed around the table and grabbed Barb by the shoulders. "You need to go cleans your aura. Try some music."

Barb squeaked and pushed him away before leaping away like a frightened cat. She shifted into her panther, which had huge chunks of fur missing. She ran to the door and clawed at it. Grace rushed over and opened it allowing her to run through. "It'll be okay, Barb," she called out.

Roman stood. "I vote for Beauregard to head our government, to get it established with the cabinet of his liking. Do I have a second?"

"Second!" Zoltar said so loudly, Wendy jumped.

"All in favor?" Roman looked around the room and every hand was raised. "Passed. Now, Grace, I would very much like you to have Xander put everything back on. There are going to be a lot of worried parents attempting to get ahold of their children. Preventing that connection may very well cost us our school. We need to make a brief announcement and assure our students it's being handled."

She nodded and looked at Xander. "Do it."

"Everyone, please return to the dining hall. I'll make the announcements and dismiss everyone to their rooms for the night." Grace's face was long. She and Roman led everyone back to the dining hall. Back at the front of the hall Grace called for everyone's attention once more.

"Most of you have heard the rumors by now. There is a group that is dead set against integration—against the thought of this very school and your right to an education. They've made a strategic move today and uploaded a video that has gone viral. They demonstrate Lycans shifting from human to wolf and back. They warn the human population we're out here and we're dangerous. I assure you we have people tasked with damage control, but be prepared. Be vigilant. When you're outside of the school grounds, take care not to shift. Take care not to let humans see you run faster, jump higher, or appear stronger than you should be. The Royals have devised a plan for us all to come out of hiding eventually, but not until we can ensure your safety. For now, there is no need to worry. You are dismissed to your dorms. Please call your families, as I'm sure if they aren't worried about you now, they will be when they catch wind of the video. Thank you."

Zoltar grabbed Wendy's hand. She gazed around at the student body. She could read confusion and fear over most of their faces, some though…didn't even look surprised.

"Let's go have a chat," she said without looking at him. She walked over to a young blonde who looked rather bored.

"Hello, Headmistress." She stood, placing her phone face down on the table.

She forced a smile. "I just wanted to walk around and make sure everyone is okay. I'm sorry, I don't recall your name?" She sniffed. The youngster was Lycan.

"I'm Brittany." The girl bowed her head slightly. Though the act appeared to be one of respect the lack of depth in the neck bow warned there wasn't as much deference there as there should be. "It's good to see you again. And I'm doing fine, I guess." Bobbing her shoulders up and down to shrug, she looked around. "I guess some of them are freaking out, huh?"

"But not you? How are you staying so calm?" Zoltar asked, squeezing Wendy's hand.

The girl plopped back on the bench. "Come on, there are shifter videos all over YouTube. This isn't the first video to surface. People get excited, and then they get bored. Humans aren't nearly as intelligent or concerned as you think. To them, we're Bigfoot. Just a myth."

"Yeah, the video will get a gazillion hits and that'll be it.

143

There might be a few blog posts but they're usually by the conspiracy whack jobs and no one pays attention to them." A young Pixie girl next to Brittany spoke up.

"Very good," Wendy nodded, though she offered a smile she felt anything but pleased. Something about the girl wasn't ringing true. When she got a chance she'd have to check future into the young woman's history. "I hope the rest of the student body shares your viewpoint. Have a good evening, Brittany."

They spoke to the other students who didn't react. They all said the same thing—it wasn't the first video to surface. What the students didn't know, was it was the first actual Lycan made video. It was real and that was cause for concern. They doubted computers could emulate the shift, the shimmering air, the molecular change. She wasn't a tech guru like Xander, but she knew film could be examined frame by frame. She'd read enough books to know as much.

She leaned into Zoltar and whispered. "I have one more person to question." Heading straight for Grace, she contorted her face into a look of concern. "Your friend Barb, is she okay? She seemed to have a mental breakdown or something."

"She's been seeing Dr. Jeffrey for a compulsive licking problem. She's cleaned most of the hair off of herself. She's very scared and nervous with the violence. Don't forget, she saw her mother murdered. She was very young and it did some damage. Perhaps you could make an effort to be friends—oh and keep this in confidence." Grace's voice in her head ended on a stern note. Barb was her friend and her emotional state was not to be the topic of rumor.

Got it.

"Had enough fun for one night?" Zoltar asked as he put his arm around her shoulder.

"More than enough." The emotional vibe in the room was draining. Students had begun filing out and it seemed like a good enough time to head back home.

Home. It had been the first time she'd thought of her living quarters as such. It had given her an unexpected feeling of happiness and belonging.

TWELVE

"Oh this is delicious. What is it?" Wendy asked as she sipped at the mug Zoltar had carried out to the fire for her.

"It's Earl Grey tea. As I promised, we are enjoying less aggressive beverages this evening. Top that with the stress of the evening and I thought a nice hot cup might be the soothing balm we needed." Sitting next to her, he eased his arm around her waist and gave a gentle squeeze.

Sipping again, she let out a breath of warm air toward the small fire. "What do you think will happen? Will we live forever in hiding or will we come out to the world, eventually?" She turned her head to get a good look at his expression, his golden hair glowing in the light of the fire, his eyes dancing with the flames.

"I get glimpses of the future. Eventually, the humans accept us. I just don't know how much damage occurs between then and now. My experiences with the humans haven't been the best. But they're so very different. Some are very accepting and intelligent. Others…not so much. The truth is, I just don't know when the right time is, but I can't say for certain that now is a good time for us. I think

146

we need to be a more cohesive society first."

"The unknown can be so frightening. But then...I look at this school. Honestly, I was nearly terrified to move. Fear of rejection and the possibility of my new pack failing to bond really had me worried. Then it hits me how protective I feel over the school and the staff. Mary is a dear friend and I'd lay my life down for her just as I would defend Grace, Roman or the herd. All of it shocks me a bit. It's happened fairly quickly. Maybe the same could be said for making ourselves known to the humans." She leaned into him, resting her head on his chest. He was warm and his mere presence always seemed to either calm her nerves or send her hormones into a fury.

After a soft kiss to the top of her head, he sighed.

"What?" she asked, sitting back to study his face.

With a smirk he shook his head. "We are a family now—the new pack, herd, whatever. It feels kind of nice."

She put her mug on the open bench next to her and turned back to face him. She reached over and scooped his hand in hers. "Before I was invited to the rooftop celebration, I had plans to bring you out here and let you know that I'm ready." Her heart felt like it was resting in her throat, the muscles constricting and causing her to swallow hard. "I'm no longer concerned about any racism we might face, rejection from the pack, or the herd. I'm ready to be bonded, if you'll still have me. I'm making this decision for myself, despite prior fears. I am taking control of myself and my future. For me, that future includes you." She took a deep breath and let it out.

Smiling, he moved his hands up to cup her face. With a slight tilt of his head, he grazed her lips with his, tracing her mouth before he finally increased the pressure with a kiss. When he released her, he gazed into her eyes. "That would make the happiest Centaur on the planet."

Running her fingers through his hair, she said, "I know you're concerned about doing this right, or rather how it works for Lycans. When we make love and our fangs begin to protrude, you bite, just a bit on the neck to draw a little blood. Then lick the wound. Your wolf will really take care of it for you, but you'll be there, conscious of the actions."

He pressed his forehead to hers. "I love that you know my concerns before I can even verbalize them."

A giggle rolled out of her throat. "That's going to get stronger after the bond."

He shot up to his feet. "Please, please, stay here. Okay? I will come back in a few minutes, but I beg you to stay here until I return."

A little startled she nodded. Instead of going back into her apartment, where they'd originated, he went through the door that led to his. She stared at the door as she finished her tea, wondering what he was up to now. He'd had some sort of idea that had hit him, caused him to jump out of his seat like he'd been shot with an arrow.

Moments later, he returned and held out a hand for her. "Come with me."

Rising to her feet, she studied him. His lips were curved into an easy smile. Taking his hand, she allowed him to lead her into his apartment.

*

Zoltar didn't care how Lycans did it. He only cared about *his* bond with *his* mate, it had to be perfect...romantic. He led her through his place to the bathroom, where the tub was filled with warm water and flower petals. He'd lit candles and arranged them around the bathroom before turning off the lights and going to retrieve her.

Her mouth fell slack as she looked at the tub. With a quick grin, he shed his clothes and helped her with hers. He eased into the giant bear claw bathtub first then held her hand as she climbed in, sitting in front of him, resting her back against his chest.

Reveling in the way the water moved, caressing her breasts as they floated in the flowered water, he kissed her neck.

She closed her eyes and leaned her head back into his collar bone. "Hmm, this is perfect, Z. A nice relaxing bath to ease our nerves."

After wrapping his arms around her and squeezing, he kissed the soft area behind her ear. "Nothing is too perfect for you. This only happens once and I want it to be memorable. We've taken the time to make the decision. We have spent time together to be certain we are meant to be. It seems foolish to rush the actual bonding."

She tilted her head and reached her hand up, running her fingers through his hair. With a gentle pull on the back of his head she brought him down to meet her in a kiss. Her silky lips caressed hers and her tongue teased his bottom lip.

Running his hands along the length of her body, he started to ache with need. *Don't rush.* He massaged her thighs as her kiss deepened. She moaned into his mouth as he kneaded her muscles. The water sloshed as she rubbed her legs together. Concerned he may be overworking her legs, he let his hands skim her body, cup her breasts then flatten out on her belly.

A gasp escaped her lips as she ceased their kiss. "I'm done with the bath." Grabbing the tub, she pulled herself off of him and to her feet. When he followed, she grabbed a fresh towel off the counter and began dabbing him dry first. She started at his shoulders and worked her way down his backside, his thighs and calves. When she moved to the front of him to dry his shins, she dropped the towel on the floor and knelt on it, swiftly moving her mouth over his erection.

He gasped when the slick warmth of her mouth enveloped him, her tongue teasing the ridge of the tip as she moved. Her hands traveled up his thighs and around to his butt as she took him deeper. He wanted to move to the bedroom, to please his woman, but her mouth felt exquisite on his aching cock.

She let his cock bob free for the briefest of moments before she ran her tongue down the shaft and licked his balls.

"That's it!" He grabbed her hands and lifted her to her feet. As soon as she was upright, he scooped one arm behind her knees and the other behind her back, lifting her into his arms. As soon as he carried her to the bed, he dove on top of her and kissed her like it would be their last, his breathing getting heavier, her breasts, still damp from the tub, pressing against his chest.

Moving his kiss from her lips to her chin then down her throat to her breasts, he fought to take his time, not to rush despite the fact that he ached to be inside of her. He moved down, licking the soft skin by her navel until he was between her legs then swooped down to taste her delicate flavor. He lapped up her lower lips, sucking them in gently until she bucked against him.

He stroked his aching cock with one hand as he rubbed her swollen clit with the other. Her legs shook and she panted. He couldn't wait any longer. Crawling up, he rested his elbows on each side of her shoulders and pushed the tip of his cock inside slowly, reveling in the delicious sensation of having her warm slick pussy accept him inch by inch until he was buried deep inside her.

After a small gasp from his love, he backed out slightly and held still for a moment, fearful of climaxing just as they were getting started. She had worked him almost to orgasm in the bathroom and it was difficult to hold on now, but she deserved his time. She deserved more than a few seconds of pleasure. Once he calmed a bit he began moving inside her.

His eyes flew open when he felt the slight pain of her teeth piercing his skin. It was only then he realized his own fangs had protruded and moved in toward her neck. With the warmth of her tongue moving over the wound, he pressed his fangs into her and did the same.

Colors of every kind flashed before his eyes. He felt her body clamp down around his cock as his own seed exploded into her. Loud clanking like steel doors echoed in his mind before raw emotion flooded him. He heard her cry out as her orgasm came in another wave.

Then his heart ached and throbbed as he felt her love, her admiration flowing through him. He saw himself through her eyes: loving, protective, gentle yet strong. Before he could process the other emotions flooding in, memories from the distant past rushed in like a tidal wave. Battles fought, female centaurs, weddings, castles, the landscape changing, his ancestors meeting with Apollo begging for mercy and more visions he couldn't handle.

He rolled to his side off of her for fear of crushing her. Blinded by the visions, he felt around until he found the edge of the comforter and pulled it up over both of them. With the blanket and a protective arm over his mate, they both remained quiet. He could only assume she was having the same experience.

"This is amazing," he heard her whisper.

He had no idea how long they'd remained still…how long the visions and memories had taken, but when his own vision returned he noticed something odd about the room. There was a faint purple glow. He looked at her, eyes were violet and glowing. Turning, he saw his own reflection and his eyes had the same hue.

She was his. He was hers. They were one.

THIRTEEN

She felt different. Her body felt different somehow, stronger. She had so many memories that had flooded in, memories from the past. The female Centaurs had been ferocious, keeping the rowdy men in check. They were strong in body, mind, and spirit. The males had been...lost without them. They spiraled out of control until their king made a plea with Apollo.

All of their emotions flooded in and she felt each and every one. Then, she felt Zoltar's feelings for her. They were so powerful, so pure. He hadn't over embellished. He had, in fact, been drawn to her from the first moment their eyes had locked...before they'd even spoken a word to each other.

She felt his elation at their bonding—pride that she was his. Hope for his herd...*their* herd.

"Z?" she whispered.

Opening his eyes, he smiled upon setting sight on her face. "Yes, my love?"

"According to Lycan tradition, we are married. We don't have to have a ceremony. But...something just occurred to me. I don't know your last name. I sort of need to know my new last name." She bit her lip. Never in a million years would she have considered a future where she bonded with a man whose surname she did not know.

"We Centaurs do not have last names. I am known only as Zoltar, son of Ethos. If you'd like to maintain your last name of Baker, I do not have any objections." Using his long fingers, he brushed the hair from her face.

With their new connection it was easy for her to know he spoke the truth. He quite literally had no feelings on the matter. The only thing mattering to him was that they were mated.

"Would you like a ceremony?"

She considered it for a moment. Years ago, it was all that was on her mind. Today? Today she didn't care. "Not really. I have all I need. I guess I just have to decide what to do about a name."

He shrugged. "Wendy, wife of Zoltar, daughter of..."

Bursting into laughter, she playfully slapped at his chest before springing out of bed. "That's a mouth full! I'll get coffee started." She went to her closet and pulled on lounge pants and a tank top before padding out toward the kitchen. She filled the brew basket with grounds and paused as a vision blinded her. The images were flashes, like spliced photos in an old film. She tried to make sense of them at first. They faded a bit and she resumed coffee preparation.

"Visions are weird, huh?" He was leaning against the door way. "Sort of blinds you for a second."

She turned and walked to him, wrapping her arms around his waist, resting her head on his chest. "Grace said it subsides."

My wolf! She remembered Grace's warning about losing contact with her wolf. *Are you there? Are you okay?* A howl made her shudder.

"Oh Goddess, that animal sounds like it's in pain." He held her a little tighter. "Are you okay?"

She took a deep breath and released it, stepping back.

153

With one firm nod she looked up at him. "I trust the queen and she said my beast will be fine."

The left side of his face twisted in a smirk. "Speaking of Queen...you bare that title now too, you know."

"I feel different, but not like royalty or anything. My body feels more...I don't know, just more." Turning she pulled out a few mugs and placed them on the counter, trying to assess exactly how she felt. Did she feel like a queen? Certainly, her idea of a royal family included wealth and castles. Standing in an apartment as part of her job as a professor didn't feel like a monarch.

What she did notice was something she already had, but more powerful. The protective feeling over the defenseless, the Gnomes and the rest of her pack and herd had only intensified.

"And you can now hear me." His voice trailed in her mind.

Keeping her back to him she grinned. *But you could have heard me all along if you wanted.*

"True, but I respected your privacy." He cleared his throat. "I only listened in on your brother, and only once when he was discussing you. He really wanted you to have a family, you know."

She spun around to face him, nearly knocking the coffee cups off of the counter. "My brother?"

"Colin is your brother, right?" He scratched his head.

"Yes, of course, just...he was *that* worried about me having a family?" She blinked a few times then shook her head, turning around to pour the coffee. "I guess I never really considered it. He did mention my lack of love life, but concern wasn't what I would have called it."

After a sip of coffee, he looked around. "So which apartment do you prefer? Yours or mine? I don't mind moving if you'd rather stay here."

Thinking about his very masculine décor, she nodded. "I'd like that very much."

Just like that, she was mated and was about to cohabitate with a mate for the first time in her life. A new sort of energy coursed through her veins making her feel jumpy, like she could run in the woods for the entire day. She really wanted her friends to know she was mated.

"I do too," he said with a wink. "Let's have a quick breakfast, clean up and go tell them."

She lifted her mug in a toast. "You in my head…that might take a bit of getting used to."

"There's one more curiosity I simply cannot wait for. Would you like to take this coffee outside and see if…if you can shift into Centaur?" The pleading look in his eyes and the hope she could feel in him was all she needed to convince her. She winked and walked without hesitation to the patio door. Once outside and her cup safely on the table, she took a few steps away onto the grass. She looked around. The only eyes on her were than of her mate's.

She focused on him, the way his legs looked while in Centaur form, his torso, lean and strong. She closed her eyes to imagine what it would feel like to walk on hooves. When she opened them again, the air around her was shimmering. She concentrated harder on what it would feel like to gallop or trot with the herd. As the shift occurred, her line of sight rose. She looked down to see long, lean legs atop golden hooves.

"I did it!" She screamed. "I did it!" She noticed something else…she was topless. Just as Zoltar was each time he shifted. But her breasts didn't appear as normal human breasts. She was covered in horse hair from slightly below the collarbone down, offering her some semblance of modesty.

"You are a magnificent specimen." A tear spilled out of his eye, running down his cheek. "I have never seen anything as beautiful."

She quickly shifted and ran to him, throwing her arms around him. "Please don't do that. No tears, okay."

He sniffed and rested his chin at the top of her head. "I will try, but I have something now I never thought possible." She heard him sniff again.

Overcome with emotion, she felt tears of her own stinging her eyes. "Come on. Let's have breakfast so we can share our news with the world!" She looped her arm in his and pulled him toward the door.

Never in her life had she slapped a breakfast together so quickly or devoured it without savoring each bite. But today, she had more pressing issues than food. Once the meal was finished, she ran off toward the shower and he left to collect fresh clothes from the home he'd be leaving.

Within half an hour they were on their way to Grace and Roman's domicile. Before Grace could knock, the door flew open.

"Oh my God!" Grace squealed. "I felt you. I felt both of you."

"I thought we were having a seizure or something." Roman joked as he walked up behind her. He held his hand out to Zoltar. "Congratulations, my friend. You couldn't have chosen a better mate. Wendy is the best."

"Yes!" Grace squeezed her again. "Yes she is. And look at your faces. You're both positively beaming! Come in! I have coffee and rolls and…just come in." She pulled her by the arm. They were nearly at a dead run by the time they reached the kitchen. Grace grabbed a coffee mug and filled it, handing it over to her. "Cream and sugar is on the table."

Wendy followed her and took a seat, gladly taking a sweet roll since her own breakfast had been rushed and haphazard. "You weren't exaggerating about the memories. That was wild. And my eyes, they're like yours."

She smiled at Roman and Zoltar as they both joined the women at the table.

"Purple is the color of royalty," Roman said with a nod. "Threw me for a loop when I saw Grace's the first time. Sort of cool, I guess."

Zoltar huffed. "Maybe for you. I'm not really used to the whole glowing eyes thing. Centaurs eyes don't glow, well, not until now anyway."

"Centaurs, yes, Grace that is the big news. I can shift into a Centaur as well." Her heart raced as she made the announcement. "It took a few minutes, but I did it."

"That makes sense if you blood bonded, you'd have some of his magic in you too. Interesting. I don't really know anyone else who has cross-bonded." Roman stroked his chin. "I guess that goes a long way toward integration." His jaw dropped and his eyes widened. "Oh fuck, I didn't mean…it's not like you're a social experiment. I totally respect your bond."

"Shut up, Roman," Wendy said with a giggle. "I know what you meant. It's okay."

Grace slugged him in the arm. "No filter!"

Roman put a roll on a plate and shoved it toward Zoltar. "Peace offering?"

Zoltar's laugh, smooth, silky like ganache, filled the room. "You can bribe me with baked goods all you want."

Leaning over and embracing Grace once again, she apologized. "I don't mean to eat and run, but we're really anxious to tell the herd."

She waved her hands at Wendy, a wide smile stuck on her face. "Go. Go! It's a great reason for a celebration."

They hurried out of the apartment.

"Herd meeting. Courtyard. Five minutes. Mandatory." His voice boomed in her mind.

He winked as they headed out of the school and onto the grounds. Centaurs galloped out of the building toward the courtyard.

"If you're going to make a scene, be seen." The air around him shimmered briefly before his large Centaur body appeared.

Her transition went faster this time, but not as fast as his. When the herd saw a female Centaur trotting toward them they started pounding their chests, with their right fists, in unison.

"May I present your Queen," he held his hand toward her.

Silence fell on the herd as they ogled her. To her own surprise, the stares and visual inspections did not cause her any discomfort. None of them had ever laid eyes on a female Centaur. Each of them circled her once then when they came around to the front of her, pounded their chest once and bowed slightly.

Love. She felt an extreme amount of love and respect for her herd. She would protect them, lead them as best she could—an oath she swore to herself.

Theron was the last to make his circle around her. When he came to the front of her, he embraced her, kissing each cheek. "May the Gods bless you and keep you."

"Gentleman, let's take our queen for her first herd run. Slow at first, allowing her time to become accustomed to her new body. When she's ready, she'll start the run." No words were spoken. The herd lined up in twos. Wendy and Zoltar at the lead, they started off at a slow trot. At first, her hooves were a bit off rhythm until she finally learned how to use all four horse legs, where were so much longer than her Lycan appendages. She took off at a slow run, the herd keeping her pace. Within minutes, she sprinted forward fast as she could. Cheers erupted behind her.

The wind on her face was exhilarating. She'd always loved running in wolf form, feeling her fur move with the breeze, but her bare skin, exposed to the air felt refreshing. Her body felt strong and graceful by the time she'd started running. Each time a hoof pounded the ground, it only solidified her feeling as Centaur, sending vibrations of belonging to her core. It would not be difficult to appreciate both forms. Both were powerful, magical, and part of her.

They made two full laps around the property before coming to rest back at the courtyard.

"She's a Queen? You've got to be kidding me!"

She and Zoltar both looked around to identify the voice they'd heard in their heads. Someone wasn't very happy about her new status. The herd, noticing something was off, circled immediately.

Her eyes caught a glimpse of the creature rounding the corner back into the building—a certain balding panther.

"Stand down," he said lifting his hand and waving it toward the ground. "Someone's feelings are a little tender today."

There had been something about Barb she didn't like from the beginning, and Grace making excuses for her did little to change that. But now, the jealous thoughts pouring out of the werecat like poison gave her more reason to be cautious. Something was definitely off about her and Wendy would get to the bottom of it.

FOURTEEN

After a brief coaching by Grace on how to tune out the thoughts of others, Wendy and Zoltar stood side by side as Grace made the introductions at the assembly. There was a loud hum of trepidation, excitement and all around nerves from most of the student body.

Tiffany, though still a student, had agreed to head the clubs the school would form.

Barb scowled during her introduction, looking as if someone had kicked her between the legs. Wendy and Zoltar both took note. Grace overheard them, shooting a look of disappointment at them both.

"I love you Grace but something is wrong with her. Keep a close eye on her." She pushed her thoughts.

Grace nodded and made her introduction.

She stepped up to the podium and looked out at the sea of eager faces. After a deep breath, she finally spoke. "You've all met me. I'm your Headmistress and Professor of Lycanthropy. I would like to personally welcome you all to McGovern University. May your first year be a successful one." She received a round of applause as she took her place next to Zoltar.

After all introductions were made, Grace dismissed them to her first class.

"She's plain and ordinary. What makes her better than me?" Barb's grousing was at near shouting levels inside her head, making her eager to put some distance between them.

Grace stepped in front of her as she tried to make her escape. "I did hear that. If I didn't hear it with my own...whatever, I would not have believed it. I'll keep my eyes and mind open."

She nodded and stepped around Grace, moving her feet at a pace quick enough to be a jog. She didn't relax until she was in her classroom addressing her students. When her phone chimed with the beginning of the period, she stood at the lectern.

"Being your first day, I don't wish to make it a difficult one. So as I hand you your books, I want you to introduce yourself." She could feel the relief washing over the students.

Each student came to her desk and retrieved their books, then turned and announced their name and home pack. She saw a familiar face approaching and it caused her smile to widen.

"Theron, son of Athos, Centaur, Belfast, Ireland herd."

Ireland? I belong to Ireland?

She'd have to discuss this with Zoltar later, but for now, she felt at ease having Theron in her class.

Approaching her now was the blonde from the dining room, the one who didn't seem phased by the video of Lycans shifting.

"Brittany Merrell, Lycan, Chicago pack." The girl lugged her books back to her desk looking bored.

Merrell? That's Grace's half-brother, Xander's, last name. Wonder if they're related?

By the time everyone had their books and made their introductions, class was nearly over. "Read the first twenty pages in Lycanthropy 101 tonight."

Numerous groans could be heard. She smiled, realizing

she'd receive the same reaction to every assignment, test, and quiz she gave them. It didn't matter, she was there to teach and they were there to learn.

This was her new life. She would lead a new generation—along with her new mate. She had a life...purpose. Even with her new royal status, she was able to continue serving others, a virtue that was as natural to her as breathing.

"How was your first class?" Her mate tossed an apple to her as he approached.

"I took it easy on them. Yours?"

Sitting on the edge of her desk, he smiled. "I'm not so nice. They have a quiz tomorrow." He cracked his neck. "I'll take it easy on them around the holidays and finals. Other than that, they'll get a rigorous year from me. There is a lot to learn about various species and some of them aren't eager to learn about the others."

"Can we talk about the elephant in the room?" She put palm on her neck.

"Grace's friend?"

She nodded. "What's her deal? You said you have a bit of precognition. Do you see anything?" Her heart rate increased as she hoped to get good news.

"Her interpersonal skills suck. I think she feels she's past due a mate. But there's something else. I agree with your assessment, something isn't right. She never thinks about her pack or any family. She's pretty much a loner, which is highly unusual for a shifter breed. She's also very money hungry and she's really pissed at Grace for making her see a doctor. She feels like Grace has abandoned her."

She stepped back, feeling her lids expand. "That's a fairly detailed assessment."

He shrugged. "I've kept an eye on that one since she bolted from the conference room. I was thinking about having a Fae or Pixie read her aura again."

Bobbing her head up and down, she agreed. "Great idea. If you do, get a reading on a Brittany Merrell as well.

She's a Lycan from the Chicago pack."

"What's up with her?"

Shrugging to give him the impression she wasn't overly concerned, she finished. "Nothing really. Just a feeling. She carries the same last name as Xander."

"Meaning?"

"His father was Jagger. Now, scoot! My next class is about to start filing in. Off you go," she said with a teasing wink.

Pressing his hand against his chest above where his heart should rest, he played as if wounded. "That hurts. That really hurts." With a playful wink, he exited her class.

* * * *

An hour long lunch is more than enough time for two newlyweds to cram in a quick meal and a lovemaking session. The moment they crossed the threshold, he scooped her up, closing the door with one foot and dashed off to the bedroom.

She grabbed the sides of his face, pulling him onto her in a deep, passionate kiss. His rough hands making quick work of pulling her skirt up. Visions of their first time together flooded her mind and she pushed them toward her mate.

"You liked that, huh?" he snickered.

"It was cruel *and* hot," she gasped, eager to have him inside her. She pulled at his shoulders, scratching his back.

The moment he got his pants below his cock, he eased it inside her. She closed her eyes and concentrated on her mate's mind. She could feel how she felt to him, her warmth and wetness hugging his cock that ached for release. She could feel him fighting not to let go so soon.

He stayed still once buried inside her, resting his forehead between her breasts as he took deep breaths. "You feel wonderful."

She smiled into his hair. "So do you. And lunchtime is

okay for quickies." A small giggle escaped her lips. "But only lunchtime."

He looked up at her, hungry eyes boring through her as pulled out and pushed into her again. She could feel every inch of him as he penetrated her to her core. She gasped with every push as her body stretched to accommodate him. She could feel him walking the line, just at the precipice of release.

The throbbing ache of her heart, filled to capacity, nearly painful in her chest, she whispered, "I love you, Zoltar."

His lips brushed against hers as he whispered his love to her, then kissed her as he moaned in climax.

After rolling to his side, he collapsed on the bed. "It's so much harder to hold back now that I can feel everything from you. It's so overwhelmingly powerful I nearly climaxed before we really started."

She kissed his chest. "That just means we need to practice at it...a lot." Twisting her lips in a devilish grin she wiggled her brows.

"We need to get cleaned up and get back. Class is in ten minutes." He moaned as he rolled off the bed. "I'd much rather stay here, practicing with you!"

"Same here." She giggled. "We have nights, weekends, holidays...we'll have to suffer through it." Having someone crave her wasn't a bad feeling at all. Her mate wanting to spend his days and nights devouring her was the sort of bond she'd always wished for.

* * * *

As the last class wrapped up a voice boomed in her head. It was Theron and he sounded...stressed. *"Herd meeting, rooftop, as soon as you can get here."*

Dismissing her last class, she wished them a pleasant evening. Slinging her bag over her shoulder she rushed toward the back hall which had the only stairs she knew of that led to the roof. Was it another attack by the separatists? Did her bond with Zoltar set them off? Racism was an ugly but powerful and dangerous mindset. Her heart raced and bile burned in her stomach, traveling up to her throat. *What if someone was hurt?*

She hustled, taking two steps at a time. When she opened the door, she gasped and jumped back, nearly falling backward down the staircase.

"Surprise!" The whole herd along with Tiffany, Grace, Roman, Mary, Ella, Beauregard, Oden and Lela were all there. There was a long banquet table, purple and white streamers and balloons and an enormous white cake on a separate table.

Grace rushed over and hugged her. "You may not want a wedding but you *will* get a celebration!" Her arms tightened around her one final time before she released her.

Her warm embrace calmed and soothed Wendy's worries.

Zoltar stepped behind Roman. "Don't hurt me!"

"You knew!" She put her hands on her hips.

Nodding he confessed, "I nearly let it slip at lunch. You were digging around in my head and…well it wasn't easy."

She tightened her lips in an attempt to hide her smile. "You're forgiven." She walked to him, pushing Roman, gently aside. Stretching up she gave him a kiss.

"Thank you, everyone. It's beautiful." She stepped back, biting her lip to keep it from quivering as she was overwhelmed by the generosity of her friends…her family.

Everyone gave their congratulations individually before she could get a good look at the cake, which had two horses resting on top that were modified with human bodies melted on top to look like Centaurs. She snickered.

"Sorry, I'm not as handy as your mate. It was the best I could do." Roman held up his fingers. "These were blistered an hour ago."

Wrapping her arms around him she attempted to hide

her tears. She'd always considered him a little brother, since he was so close to Colin. He'd always been around. Trying to melt together Centaur cake toppers by far the sweetest thing she'd ever witnessed from him.

During dinner, she frequently caught her mate staring at her and smiling. "What? Why do you keep grinning at me like that? You look goofy." She snickered.

"Just in disbelief I have such a beautiful bride. Allow me a little goofiness tonight?" Forcing his bottom lip out made him look even sillier.

She laughed and shook her head. "Carry on."

"Wendy," Mary interrupted, her tiny little face turned up, tiny teeth shining. "I thought you'd like to know your friends Nala and Colin have taken in almost thirty of my people. More are coming. I don't know the details, but they have found a way to support themselves and contribute to the pack." She put her hands together and held them above her heart. "Isn't that wonderful?"

Already in a state of euphoria, she directed her smile at Mary, feeling a sense of pride in her idea. "It is wonderful. I'm really happy for you and the rest of the Gnomes. Hopefully this will mean a more peaceful and comfortable existence."

Mary handed her a napkin to dab away the tears.

As soon as the plates were cleared the cake was served. At the same time, the sun fell below the tree line and Gustav joined the party...with a guest. On his arm, looking the best she had in years was Michelle, Grace's long lost mother.

"Michelle! You look wonderful." She hugged her and kissed her on the cheek.

"So do you. I'm so very happy for you Wendy." A tear welled up in her eye. "A mate! I wish nothing but happiness and many little Wendy's in your future."

She released Michelle and embraced Gustav, keeping her promise to him. If vampires could thaw, she'd swear he melted into her.

"Many best wishes, Wendy. You deserve all of the happiness the world has to offer." His cool lips brushed her cheek.

The celebration lasted another hour before everyone returned home for the night. Wendy and Zoltar walked hand in hand toward their newly shared home. "That was a very nice surprise." Her gaze fell on the floor before her as they strolled down the hall.

"I'm so relieved. You said you didn't want an official wedding, but our friends thought there should be some form of celebration." He squeezed her hand.

Her cheeks, sore from smiling, pulled her lips into an enormous smile. "Our marriage is definitely worth celebrating."

When she opened the door her jaw dropped. Dozens of vases of flowers littered her entire living space. Roses, lilies, azaleas, and carnations were nicely arranged on every surface imaginable.

"Too much?" He whispered from behind her.

She stared a moment longer before turning around, mouth slack. "I'd say! When did you have time to do this?" Looking down she noticed there was a trail of rose petals leading to the bedroom.

"Follow the trail." His voice was low, primal, sending tingles up her spine.

She followed the trail of rose petals to the bedroom where the bed was also adorned with petals and something else…silk ties placed neatly in rows at the foot of the bed.

"With this new connection of ours, I don't have to worry if I'm going too far because I'll hear it, I'll feel it. Still, I'd like you to tell me if you want to stop, okay?" Standing behind her, kissing her neck, he wrapped his arms around her.

Closing her eyes, she leaned back into him, running her hands along his thick, lean thighs. With nimble fingers, he pulled her shirt over her head and while her arms were raised, ran his fingers along the tender flesh inside her arms, down her sides, then back up again, this time, unclasping her bra.

Heartbeat loud in her ears, she turned around to face him. Stretching up on her toes, she locked her fingers behind his neck, pulling him down for their lips to move in a lovers' kiss. Teasing his bottom lip with her tongue, he opened his mouth slightly. She loved kissing him. He knew how to just brush his tongue lightly across her mouth instead of trying to cram it in. It was always tender, even when it was rushed with urgent need.

Breaking the kiss long enough to remove his own shirt, he then lifted her and placed her back against the rose petal covered bed. Her eyes began to glow, she noticed as his face was lightly illuminated.

"That's going to take some getting used to." He smiled then kissed the hollow of her collar bone. Sitting up, he scooped two silk ties in his hand. He moved beside her, kissing his way from her shoulder to her wrist before he bound one to the headboard. The tie was tight, but not uncomfortable. He repeated the same procedure with the other arm until both arms were tied above her head.

With her hands bound she was totally vulnerable. What happened now would be choreographed by him and she would enjoy the ride, of that she was certain.

He pulled her skirt and panties under her bottom, slowly down her thighs and over her ankles, tossing them to the floor leaving her completely naked. He edged up toward her head. "Turn your head away from me, please."

Confused, she looked at him for a moment before looking away. She felt the pins holding her hair, sliding out. He spread her hair out over the pillow, fanning it a bit. "You have the most beautiful hair," he whispered.

With anticipation, she watched as he picked up another piece of silk, this time it looked like a long scarf. Suspending it above her, he brushed it against the skin of her shins, then thighs, pausing at her mound. He gently pushed her legs apart slightly and slid his elbow onto the mattress between her knees. He pulled the silk tight and rubbed it against the lips of her pussy, the soft, silky material gently caressing her clit. With a devilish grin, he placed his hand around her ankle pushing it up toward her thigh.

She enjoyed not knowing what was coming next. She enjoyed relinquishing total control. It drove her excitement to levels she'd not yet experienced. He began fastening the scarf to her ankle, then thigh, securing them together.

"That's not too tight?"

She shook her head and bit her lip as he repeated the same knotting procedure, binding her free ankle to its corresponding thigh. She could only close her legs using her hip muscles now. When he picked up yet another silk tie she could not imagine what there was left to bind.

"What is that for?" she gasped, her heart now racing out of control.

He only gave a soft chuckle as he used it first to tickle her flesh, draping it across her belly, then gliding it across, inching up to her breasts. When he dragged it across her nipples, they stretched and rose to the stimulation, a slight tickle, a little tingle and a whole lot of heat, she gasped, hoping his warm, soft lips would be suckling on them soon.

Another sly grin flashed at her as he looped the fabric around both breasts then tugged on it, cinching her breasts together, so that they both stood erect at the center of her chest. He tied a knot, securing the fabric before finally teasing her left nipple with his tongue.

"Absolutely breathtaking." He sat and stared down at her.

"And totally vulnerable," she teased wanting him to say or do something. Her need for him was at building to a point at bursting.

Standing from the bed, he dropped his pants, setting his erection free. When he knelt on the bed next to her head, she needed no instruction. Obediently, she opened her mouth, welcoming his cock into it. He moaned as he slowly eased himself in and out of her mouth. She tried to take more of him, but he'd only allow her slightly more than the tip.

He stretched his arm out and tweaked her nipple, causing ripples of pleasure and need to her pussy. She moaned and opened her legs, hoping to entice him. Retreating from her mouth, he crawled down the bed retrieving yet another length of silk, this time he wrapped it around his own hand, covering it entirely. With the slightest pressure, and using his silken hand he ran over the length of her body, igniting every nerve.

Moving to his knees between her legs, he pressed his warm lips on her pussy. Her body, quivering with need, bucked against him, aching for more pleasure. With torturous slow speed, he sunk a finger in her, massaging her core while his warm wet tongue swirled around her swollen bud.

She moved below him rocking her hips, dancing at the precipice of orgasm. Her breasts felt as if they were filled and about to burst. Her pussy quivered as she silently begged for just a bit more of him. She pulled at the silken tethers holding her still to the bedframe.

"Z, please!"

A low, soft chuckle vibrated against her pussy and he gave her just a bit more pressure with his tongue and another finger slid inside her. Her body instantly clamped around it as she was blinded by an explosion of color as she rode her wave of ecstasy, finding her relief.

He brought her legs together then moved them to her left side. Sitting up on his knees, he dragged the head of his cock along her slippery slit, lubricated by her orgasm. She gasped as he entered her, her core still ignited from orgasm. He squeezed the flesh along her hip as he thrust again and again. But he stopped short of reaching his peak and moved her, so her legs were open again.

She gasped when he straddled her chest and stared at

her tits, devilish grin painted on his face. With her breasts tied together, he slipped his cock under the fabric and between her breasts. She could see the image in his mind…exactly what he wanted. Opening her mouth, she offered a warm mouth for the tip of his cock as she pushed himself between her breasts.

"Oh!" He pulled back and cupped his hand over the tip of his cock to avoid coating her in his seed before collapsing on the bed next to her. Still shaking and trying to catch his breath, he started untying her bindings. Once she was free, he tossed the scarves aside and cradled her, pulling her head to his chest and wrapping his arms around her shoulders.

Overcome with euphoria, she started to giggle. "I rather enjoy being tied up. Who knew?"

He squeezed her. "I did, well, I thought." His lips pressed against her forehead. "You're magnificent. I can honestly say I've never enjoyed making love as much as I do with you. This connection we have is wonderful and terrible at the same time. Feeling you nearing climax makes it terribly difficult for me to hold on."

"Yes, but getting a visual of your desires makes it fun. I don't have to wonder what you want, I just know." She kissed his chest and snuggled in.

He was all hers. She was finally half of a whole…and it was more fulfilling than she imagined. Having a partner who anticipated her needs, what she might even desire was beyond what she expected.

FIFTEEN

It didn't take long for them to fall in sync with their new life. Classes during the day, meals and runs with the herd and other pack members at night. Her friendship with Mary continued and they'd meet a few times a week after classes.

It wasn't the life she'd dreamed of—she could never have imagined it. But it was better than a dream, it was her reality.

The prisoner in the basement was treated well, while they decided what to do with him and those like him. What would the punishment be...death? Confinement? They couldn't allow him to go back to harming others.

Beauregard held a meeting where he outlined the new government and appointed representatives of each species. Every species, down to the Gnomes had an equal vote for the equality of all. An old jail had been purchased to house supernaturals, though it needed modification. He'd also managed to establish a research facility so they could all understand themselves a bit better. He'd been the perfect person for the job.

They were on their way to existing as a civilized society.

It wouldn't be long before they could safely come out to the humans. An opportunity that seemed more and more likely, with each meeting they held.

Wendy stretched out on the couch, feeling unusually tired after a long day. Zoltar brought her a cup of Earl Grey tea which had quickly become her favorite. She closed her eyes and took a sip of the steaming brew. An acrid taste assaulted her tongue.

"Ew," she complained then sniffed the mug. "Does tea go bad?" She took another sip. "Oh, yuk!" She put the cup on the table and ran to the bathroom where she not-so-quietly lost her lunch. *Oh God! I've been poisoned. They finally got to me.* She rushed back out to the living room to see her mate sniffing her mug.

"Don't drink that! It could be poisoned!"

"There's nothing wrong with…" His eyes rose to meet hers as his mouth fell agape.

They both froze.

"Oh shit!" She grabbed her stomach. "Oh! Z!"

Alligator tears quickly formed in his eyes as he stared at her for a brief moment. He returned the cup to the table as he ran up to her, sniffed her then scooped her up. "I'm going to be a father!" He twirled her in a circle, nauseating her further.

"Put me down. Stop! Put me down," she begged, worried she'd paint the walls with whatever was left in her stomach.

He gently put her back on the floor. "I'm sorry. I wasn't thinking."

She could feel the tears stinging her eyes. "I'm finally gonna…we're gonna be parents." She sobbed into his chest, overwhelming joy knocking the wind out of her. He squeezed her. "Let's get you back to the couch and get something on your stomach."

We are with child! He pushed his thoughts toward the herd. Almost immediately there was a knock at the door. Of all the creatures in the castle, Barb stood outside their home.

"I, uh, was standing next to a very excited Centaur who apparently received a message from you." She held out a bottle of ginger ale and a package of crackers. "My sister used this when she was pregnant." After shoving them into Zoltar's hands, she began to run away.

"Come back!" Wendy yelled. She waited until the woman reappeared. She waved her in. "Thank you, Barb." When the woman stood, staring at her feet, Wendy felt something—sadness. "Barb, please come in."

The werecat came in and sat, folding her hands in her lap and staring at the floor.

She looked at her mate, who tightened his lips and nodded. He retrieved a glass of ice and brought it along with the ginger ale and crackers to her. "I'm going to meet with the herd. I'll be back soon." After kissing her on the forehead, he left.

As soon as the door was closed, she poured the glass of ale and sipped at it. "How are you? I know this year has been difficult for you with all of the stress."

She could feel waves of frustration coming off her guest. "I'm managing."

"Do you want to tell me what's going on with you? I'm not Dr. Jeffrey, but I am a good listener." She tore the package of crackers open and took a bite, choking it down. It tasted dirty, felt like sandpaper but it did settle her stomach.

"I don't want to. I just... I can't." Her bottom lip trembled.

She wasn't going to open up, but something was clearly eating at her. Maybe it wasn't that Barb was hiding something sinister...but Wendy considered the werecat might be suffering. She pushed her mind out to Barb's searching, listening.

"I'm a mutt. Who on earth is going to accept a mutt? You won't understand. You can't."

"You should never think of yourself as a mutt!"

Barb's mouth fell open and her eyes widened as she finally looked her in the eye. "How?"

"I can hear your thoughts, something that might be helpful to Dr. Jeffrey. Barb, you're not a mutt. That's a horrible thing to think."

She put her face in her hands and sobbed. "I have never had a herd, a pack, a pride or a flock. My parents were mixed breeds that got together and made a mess when they made me. It's so lonely. I mean really, did you believe I couldn't smell Grace a mile away?"

Suddenly the entire picture came into focus. Barb had lied to Grace for years, had hid her own identity, hopeful that Grace would pick up on it, but the poor thing never knew she was a Lycan until Roman and Colin went to claim her.

"You know, Z isn't full blooded Centaur. None of them are. I'd venture to say most of them are mixed with many different species. You have a place here, Barb. *We* are your pack. *All* of us. But you're carrying around a lot of guilt and mixed emotions. I suggest you go find Grace and be honest with her. Remember, she spent over twenty-years thinking she was human. I can't think of anyone else other than Z who would understand how you feel." She grabbed Barb's hand and held onto it. "Now I know why I didn't trust you. I picked up on your deception, but couldn't put my finger on it. With so many scents from so many species it all becomes cloudy."

Barb moved in closer to her and put her arms around her, crying on her shoulder. "I needed this so badly."

She squeezed. "I'm sorry, oh, I'm—" She ran into the bathroom, losing the crackers and soda. "Damn."

"It gets better," Barb handed a damp cloth to her with a smile that oozed pity. "As I said, my late sister was sick for about a month, and then said she felt the best she ever had. Something about pregnancy really makes you feel alive. At least that's what she said."

She leaned back on her heels. "Thank you. But I'd

prefer you go. I really don't want anyone to see me this way. And again, many thanks for the crackers and soda. Please, go talk to Grace." Her skin was so hot it felt like it would burst into flames. She could feel the dampness of sweat in her hair.

After a quick bob of her head, she left. Wendy flattened out on the cool tile which seemed to douse the flames. She shifted to wolf so she could use all four paws to carry her back to the couch before shifting back. The shift had actually cured her of the nausea long enough to get some more crackers and soda down.

Moving her hand down over her lower stomach, she smiled. A month of nausea would be worth it. Her first child was on its way. Her first child, with her new mate…how quickly life had changed.

THE END

SNEAK PEEK, CHAPTER ONE, NO QUARTER, BOOK 3

Chapter One

Nala Baker took her job as the first female Alpha seriously. A serious responsibility that meant she had to be sharp physically as well as mentally. She bent at the waist, touching her toes, feeling her muscles stretching. After standing straight, she grabbed the front of her ankle and stretched her leg behind her, then repeated with her other leg before she set off down the trail, first at a slow jog.

The early morning light peered through the trees, shooting golden beams on the path before her. The cool morning air brushed against her face, cooling her body which heated up quickly during runs. Morning dew sparkled in the light, causing her face to twitch into a smile. The forest was waking. The sweet earthy aroma amplified by the dew was sweet in her nose.

It was only a matter of time before some male showed up and challenged her for her spot. It could be a member of her own pack. When they did, they'd pay for that mistake. She swore the day she took the life of her last abusive male Alpha, she'd never have a man in charge of her life again. She'd die first.

As each foot took its turn pounding against the forest floor, her heart thundered in her chest. Her thighs began to burn as she picked up the pace. She claimed the forest in her mind, obsessed over every small detail of pack business. The farmers' production began to increase with a few suggestions by Tiffany, a pack member who was attending McGovern University, the first university exclusively for supernatural students.

Things were going well. Her arranged marriage to Colin was still stiff. They'd held hands, exchanged pleasantries and had even taken to quick pecks on the cheek when greeting or departing each other. They'd yet to take their relationship any further. It was an internal struggle for them both. Colin, still grieving his late wife and child and Nala, a victim of heinous acts of her former Alpha hadn't been ready to consummate the relationship.

But Nala wanted more than a friendly business arrangement. Though she'd never admit it to anyone else, she mourned that special bond she'd never had. She wanted to enjoy sex again. She'd have to be vulnerable to her mate, yet seem completely invulnerable to everyone else. That was a riddle she'd yet to solve.

She reached her favorite tree, with a nice level branch, leaped up and grabbed it with both hands. She pulled herself up, lifting her chin above the branch, then lowering herself until her arms were fully extended. She repeated the movement twenty-four more times, reveling in the burn rippling through her biceps and shoulders before she dropped back to the ground and commence her run.

Five more minutes and she'd reach the main house. Slowing her pace slightly, she considered the Gnomes. Wendy Baker, Colin's sister, had requested the Belfast pack to take the little people in. They needed protection so they didn't have to live like rodents and in return, they would work around the pack contributing in any way they could.

It seemed like a fair arrangement. Tiny houses were built among the Lycan houses. Two dozen little homes butted up to larger ones that offered protection from the elements.

In return, farmers had help milking cows, feeding chickens, and collecting eggs. The Gnomes had an enormous garden they tended with herbs and vegetables they distributed among the pack. Some of them had taken to child care, or HVAC work, running or repairing duct work in what would be cramped attic space to a Lycan. Two of the Gnomes were experts and locating, cutting and polishing jewels and had taken to selling extravagant jewelry, mostly to the Vampires, who were fond of such baubles. Though Nala had been wary of taking on what she thought would be an extra responsibility, so far the relationship had been quite symbiotic.

Zoltar, Wendy's new mate and the Centaur King, and his men had begun manufacturing small automobiles for the Gnomes so they could get around more easily. Little jeep-like vehicles with fat tires to maneuver among rocks and branches carried the little people all over the property.

Jake, Colin's half-brother and look-alike had been selected as her Beta. It was a less than popular decision for the women who came with her from the Scottsboro pack, but she had to blend the two packs together and Jake was a nice bridge between the old regime and the new. He was also effective and loyal, two qualities Nala appreciated.

She finally reached the main house and stopped, taking a moment to gain her composure before entering the house, which was always buzzing with Lycans first thing in the morning. Closing her eyes, she tilted her face toward the sun, reveling in the warmth of the rays licking at her skin.

"I, uh, brought you a glass of water."

She opened her eyes and watched as Colin approached holding a glass in his hand. She found him handsome the first time they'd met. When he was nervous, he'd trip on his tongue or run his fingers through his thick wavy blond locks.

"That was thoughtful. Thank you." With a smile she grabbed the glass out of his hand and took a long drink, thankful to have the cool water running down her throat, which was hot and dry from her run. He always seemed to attempt to take care of her in some manner, just like bringing her a glass of water after her morning run.

"Breakfast is almost ready." He stared at her for two seconds more than was comfortable before turning on his heel and heading back into the house.

Would the awkwardness ever go away?

Releasing a breath she hadn't realized she was holding, she followed him into the house. Maybe she should make the first move. Maybe she should plan an intimate dinner. Maybe...she didn't know what the hell she was doing.

She took her usual seat at the head of the table with Colin sitting to her right and Jake, her Beta, sitting to her left. The two men often exchanged uncomfortable glances with each other and while it ate at Nala, the not knowing what the looks were about, she couldn't bring herself to ask her mate if there was a problem. Maybe it was because Colin was the former Alpha of the Belfast pack and his current position as her advisor was in conflict with her having a Beta whose job it was to be her right hand man. Maybe it was sibling rivalry. Whatever it was made her squirm in her chair. The tension was nearly palpable.

She sipped at her coffee then cut into her Country Fried Steak, appreciating the wonderful food she enjoyed instead of the slop she'd been fed in the not-so-distant past. Dipping a biscuit into the gravy she glanced around and watched her pack mates as they smiled and conversed over breakfast. The only place there didn't seem to be harmony was her little corner of the table, with the mate she'd yet to bond with and his half-brother.

"I was thinking," she started, in an effort to break the tension, "maybe we can put some crushed stone paths down for the Gnomes' cars. I know their little cars get them around but it has to be a bumpy ass ride around this terrain."

Jake pulled out a small pad of paper he kept in his front pocket and jotted it down. "I'll get some quotes." He tucked the paper back into the pocket and continued eating.

It took every ounce of control for her not to roll her eyes. "Colin, I was thinking about going into town today. Would you care to join me?" She placed her fork on her plate and folded her hands in her lap. When she turned to him she found him beaming at her, his smile wide.

"I'd like that very much."

Her heart fluttered. She returned his smile and nodded. "By the time I'm cleaned up and finish some paperwork, it'll be nearly lunch. Maybe we can have lunch in town?"

He slid his hand across the table and placed his hand on hers, giving a gentle squeeze. "That sounds perfect." Scooting back from the table, he dropped his napkin on his chair and left the dining room.

She watched the back of him as he left, his head held a little higher than when he brought her the water. He even seemed to have a bit of a spring in his step.

Returning her focus back to the table, she caught the end of Jake rolling his eyes.

"Something on your mind?" she crossed her arms over her chest and narrowed her eyes.

"Not a thing." He jerked his chair back and tossed his fork down on his plate before making his own quick departure.

Men.

"Thank you for the breakfast, Trace." She smiled at Tracy, her most trusted female companion and who she'd intended to be her Beta before coming to the Belfast pack. Tracy had handled it well, insisting on her desire for peace being greater than any need for position. She now managed the house, which was a far cry from Beta duties.

She hated seeing her friend stuck in a traditional domestic role, but Tracy didn't seem to mind too much.

After excusing herself she made her way to room. She kicked off her shoes and walked into the bathroom, peeling off her clothes. She turned on the shower and stepped in, closing her eyes as the water poured over her. She had to think of a reason to go into town. It was a spur of the moment decision to spend some time with her mate. But now, she needed an excuse. What would they do once they arrived? Where, exactly, would they go?

She tried to concoct a plan as she lathered her hair with soap. Nothing came to mind. Jake took care of ordering supplies. Tracy had always made sure they were well stocked with feminine products. She could use some clothes. She hadn't come with much and what little she had was wearing thin. The Alpha shouldn't dress like a bum, but would Colin be bored out of his mind shopping for clothes?

Of course he would, he was a man.

She sighed. It was the only excuse she could devise.

After a quick conditioning of her hair and a good scrub she was rinsed and drying off.

"Uh, Nala?" Colin called through the door.

Her heart jumped into her throat. He hadn't seen her naked yet and this was not how she wanted it to go. "I'll be out in a moment," she called out, throwing her robe on and cinching it closed.

"Oh, hi." He looked away when she opened the door. "I just…uh…was wondering…Um…You didn't say what we were doing in town. Do I need to get the truck ready?"

She felt a smirk forming on her face as she tried to hide her amusement. "Colin?"

He looked at her. "I don't want you to think, you know, that I was trying to catch you in the shower or anything. I came to get my wallet and heard you in there."

She let go of a chuckle. "It's okay. We don't need the truck. I actually need some clothes and we always have everyone around here watching us so closely. I thought it might be nice for us to spend some time together while not being under a microscope. I hope clothes shopping won't be too much of a drag for you."

He lifted his chin. "I happen to have excellent taste in women's' apparel. I was considering getting a new pair of heels myself."

She nearly gasped when he winked at her. He'd only done it a few times before. He'd always seemed to flirt with her when she least expected it, but never really when she did.

"Well, not in red. It would clash with your eyes."

His throaty laugh made her heart ache. He really needed to laugh more. When he smiled it made his eyes squint a little at the sides. He had a sweet boyish look to him when he laughed. It was endearing and very rare, at least in her experience.

"Okay then. I'll just go. See you in a bit." Before she could do or say anything else, he made a quick exit.

She walked over to the bed and sat on the edge. Her heat was coming soon and she certainly didn't want their first time to be during a heat. With a heavy heart she walked into her closet to dressed, her eyes falling to the note she found this morning hidden under her coffee cup. It's pasted lettering warning her; *enjoy your power while you can female alpha...it's about to end!*

Other Books by Anita Cox

<u>Dirty White Candy Series</u>
<u>The Beginning, Book 1</u>
<u>Ultimate Vacation, Book 2</u>
<u>Trading Places, Book 3</u>

<u>Shifter Chronicles</u>
<u>Pursuing Grace, Prequel</u>
<u>Saving Grace, Book 1</u>
<u>Resurrection, Book 2</u>
<u>No Quarter, Book 3 (Coming Summer, 2015)</u>